THE DISCOVERY OF MAGIC

ELEMENTALS ACADEMY

BOOK ONE

MICHELLE MADOW

DREAMSCAPE PUBLISHING

THE DISCOVERY OF MAGIC
Elementals Academy 1

Published by Dreamscape Publishing

Copyright © 2022 Michelle Madow

ISBN: 9798406742471

For Claire, for being with me through this crazy/fun/challenging journey of being an indie author for the past six years, and for becoming one of my best and most supportive friends in the process.

CHAPTER ONE

C ome have dinner with us in the dining hall!
The text from one of my friends buzzed on my phone.

"Who's that?" my best friend Lara asked.

"One of the girls from my book club," I said. "Inviting me to dinner in the dining hall."

"Oh," Lara said, since we both knew what my answer had to be.

Just like me, Lara was a scholarship student. And since living in the dorms was expensive, it worked out perfectly for us to rent an apartment together.

It was far cheaper than living on campus. But it also had its downsides.

Already had dinner, I replied. Can't wait to see you at book club next week!

I frowned, then pressed send.

Because by the time I got in my car and drove to campus, they would have already finished their meal.

The truth was that I hadn't had dinner yet. Lara and I were currently sitting out on our balcony, drinking wine and chatting as we enjoyed the perfect January weather. Because in Florida, summer was so hot that it feels like you're drowning in a steam room season, and winter was the it's comfortable enough to wear a light sweatshirt and not feel like you're burning in the fiery pits of Hell season.

Lara poured herself another glass of the cheap white wine we were drinking, then checked my glass, disappointed to see it was half-full. "Cheers to being the poor kids on campus," she said, and we both drank to that. "Anyway, what's going on with the hot senior guy you're tutoring in English?"

"You mean Trent?"

"Obviously."

"His essays are getting better." I shrugged. "I might be able to help him get a C for the semester."

"That's not what I meant." Lara rolled her eyes. "What's going on with *you* and him?"

"Wait," I said. "You think I'd actually be *interested* in Trent? As in, want to date him?"

Lara knew me better than that. Preppy, party-boy

jocks who were almost failing English and had probably never read a book for fun in their life were about as far from my type as you could get.

"It's not me who thinks it," she said. "I overheard his girlfriend talking to a friend in the library about it today."

"Courtney?"

He'd mentioned Courtney a lot last semester. The perfect sorority girl he'd been dating for the past three years.

"The one and only president of Kappa Kappa Beta," she said, and I rolled my eyes.

Those sorority girls took themselves *way* too seriously.

"I'm just a freshman who tutors Trent twice a week," I said. "I'm surprised Courtney even knows I exist."

"Oh, she *knows* you exist," Lara said. "And she thinks you're after her boyfriend."

"Well, she has nothing to worry about," I said. "Trent's never been anything more than friendly around me."

Although now that I was thinking about it, he hadn't mentioned Courtney since school had started back up this semester.

"You sure about that?" she asked.

"Yes, I'm sure," I said. "And I doubt I'm his type."

"You underestimate how hot you are," Lara said. "You're *any* guy's type. At least, any guy who isn't blind."

"They sure have a funny way of showing it."

Sure, I noticed guys checking me out sometimes. But none of them had ever gotten to the point where they wanted to talk to me, let alone get to know me.

"Because you're intimidating," she said, and then she placed her wine glass down on the arm of her chair and dramatically continued. "Shiny black hair that shampoo models would kill for, perfect skin, and green eyes that I still don't believe aren't color contacts, even though we've known each other since we were eleven."

"Or they just see me as that weird girl who likes books more than people, and then they move on to someone more fun."

"You're fun!" she said. "Anyone who doesn't think so clearly doesn't know the real you."

"You're the only person who knows the 'real me,'" I muttered, since this was far from the first time we'd had this conversation. "And my mom. But I don't think she counts."

"It's because you don't let your guard down," she said. "And—like I said—you're intimidating."

"Not to you."

"Only because the first time we spoke, you asked me what my Harry Potter house was," she said, and she lifted her feet to rest them on the balcony, picking her wine glass back up and leaning back into her chair. "Before then, I was definitely intimidated."

"Spoken like a true Ravenclaw," I said.

"Hey." She smiled and raised her glass. "Ravenclaws are the best."

We clinked our glasses, and I took a sip, looking out over the balcony at our "luxurious" parking lot view.

Suddenly, green, swirling lights with some purple and pinks mixed in exploded in the night sky.

Lights that looked just like the *Northern Lights*.

In Florida.

I blinked, as if they'd go away, but they were still there.

"No way," Lara said, breathless. "Are those the Northern Lights?"

I sucked in a sharp breath as magnetic energy hummed through my body. The wind chimes hanging from the ceiling clanged against each other, going absolutely nuts even though the air was still.

"Summer?" Lara asked to get my attention.

"I think so," I said, and then the colorful lights disappeared as quickly as they'd arrived. The wind chimes stopped clanging, too.

"But you can only see those in Norway." She looked to me like *I'd* have the answer.

"And other places in the Arctic." I picked up my

phone and scrolled through social media, reading the posts that were popping up on my feed. "Other people saw it, too."

"I'd hope so," she said. "Otherwise, something seriously freaky would be going on."

"We just saw the Northern Lights in Florida," I said. "Something freaky's already going on."

She pressed her lips together, deep in thought. "Maybe it has to do with global warming," she eventually said.

"Maybe," I said, although that explanation didn't feel *right*. "Did you feel something strange while we watched them?"

"What sort of 'something strange'?"

"A buzzing feeling. Like electricity traveling through your body?"

"No." She eyed me like I'd lost it. "Did you have too much wine?"

"Half a glass."

"And when was the last time you ate?"

"Hm." I thought back over my day. I'd spent lunchtime in the library, making flashcards for an Art History test coming up in two days. "I had half a sandwich at lunch."

"Not enough," she said. "And we're definitely gonna be up all night looking out for more Northern Lights and searching online to figure out what's going on. We need brain food. Want to order pizza?"

"Definitely." I opened the app on my phone, placed our typical order, then looked back up at the sky.

It was just as normal as ever.

Lara was on her phone, tapping frantically.

"Find anything?" I asked.

"Other than a bunch of crazy theories like aliens descending onto the planet to take over the world?" she said. "No."

I eyed my phone, which I'd placed down next to me. Maybe I should call my mom. This was the sort of thing she lived for. She'd probably have some mystical theory as crazy as the alien invasion one Lara had found online.

Just as I was thinking about it, my phone rang.

My mom.

I picked it up. "Hey," I said, bracing myself for whatever was coming.

"I'm assuming you saw it?" she asked.

"You mean the Northern Lights in Florida?" It was impossible to keep the sarcasm out of my tone.

"Of course that's what I mean," she snapped, which took me by surprise, since she was one of the calmest people I knew.

"You okay?" I asked.

"Something isn't right," she said. "I want you to come home."

"I can't come home," I said, since it was a three-hour

drive I didn't have time to make. "I have a test on Friday."

"Tell your teacher there's a family emergency."

"I'm not missing the first test of the semester," I said, although I felt bad, given how frantic she sounded. "I can come home Friday afternoon after I'm done taking the test. Okay?"

She said nothing for a few seconds.

"Okay," she said slowly, although she didn't sound happy about it. "Call me when you leave."

"Will do," I said. "Bye."

Lara watched me curiously. "What was that about?" she asked after I ended the call.

"My mom's being weird." I glanced at my phone, feeling more uneasy by the second.

"Your mom's always weird," Lara said, since as my best friend since sixth grade, she was the only person on Earth who could say that without being offensive. "But she sounded totally freaked out. Are you really going home on Friday?"

"I have to," I said, my mom's frantic tone running through my mind again. "Hopefully it'll only be for a night."

"Hm," she said, and then she said the absolute *last* thing I expected. "Can I come with you?"

I waited for her to say she was kidding.

She didn't.

"Are you sure?" I asked. "She'll probably have us do a meditation circle on the beach to re-align our chakras or something."

"The Northern Lights just happened in Florida, and no one knows why," she said. "Maybe a chakra re-alignment session will do me some good."

"I think I'd believe you more if you said you agreed with the people who think we're being invaded by aliens."

"Anything's possible now," she said. "And whatever your mom wants to do probably beats anything going on around here."

She sounded casual about it, but from the way she glanced warily out at the parking lot, I had a feeling she didn't want to be left in the apartment alone.

"I'll ask her. If she says yes, then of course you can come," I said, and then my stomach growled so loudly that she could hear it.

"See?" She pointed at my stomach. "You need to eat. But in the meantime…" She picked up the wine bottle and held it out to me.

"Weren't you just giving me a hard time about what a lightweight I am on an empty stomach?" I asked.

"You're always a lightweight—empty stomach or

not," she said. "But the sky's going crazy, and the apoca-lypse might be near. The least we can do is have another drink."

"Fair point," I said, and then I held out my glass and let her fill it to the top.

CHAPTER TWO

Even though the sky had gone crazy last night, classes still went on as normal.

At lunchtime, I walked to the building across the dining hall and walked down the steps to the off-campus student lounge. It always smelled musty, and the furniture was decades old. It was nowhere near as bright and airy as the other buildings on campus—like the lounge in itself was trying to say that scholarship students didn't belong at an expensive private college.

A few of my acquaintances were huddled around the TV, watching news coverage on the Northern Lights.

The lights had happened across the half of the world where it had been nighttime. Scientists were baffled, and conspiracy groups were continuing to go nuts with their theories.

But instead of joining the group by the TV, I walked to one of the study tables at the other side of the room and started chowing down on the sandwich I'd brought from home, wanting to be finished eating before Trent arrived for our tutoring session.

"Summer Donovan," someone said from behind me.

I put the remaining half of my sandwich down at the sound of my name, then turned around and saw none other than the president of Kappa Kappa Beta—Courtney herself. She was petite, and her blond hair was so perfectly curled that she'd probably spent an hour on it before going to her first class. Instead of a backpack, she carried a black Chanel bag just big enough to fit her laptop.

Her expression was totally neutral and un-readable.

"Hi." I squirmed a bit in my chair, ready for her to question me about my time with Trent.

It's going to be okay, I told myself. *Nothing's going on with Trent. I'll be honest with her, and then she'll leave.*

Before I could continue my over-thinking, she pasted a friendly smile onto her face. "I know Trent has his session in ten minutes, so I'll make this quick," she said. "Rush week just ended, and I didn't see you there."

"You mean sorority rush?" I asked.

"Of course!" She laughed, as if the question was ridiculous.

Had the Northern Lights sent me into some alternate universe where Courtney cared if I attended sorority rush week or not?

I didn't really think that, but *that* was how crazy it was that she was asking me this.

"You didn't see me there because I'm not rushing a sorority," I said slowly.

She squared her shoulders and widened her smile. "Well, I think you'd be a great fit for Kappa," she said. "Which is why I came here—to invite you to have dinner with us tonight so the girls can meet you and see if we want to offer you a snap bid!"

I stared at her like she'd lost her mind and waited for some kind of punchline.

There apparently wasn't one.

"Why do you think I'm a 'great fit for Kappa'?" I asked, unintentionally mocking her bubbly tone.

It was hard not to.

If she'd noticed, she didn't show it.

"Trent's said such great things about you. I thought it would be nice if you stopped by to meet the girls." She looked around and lowered her voice, like she was making sure no one was listening. "And truthfully, we both know he wouldn't have passed English last semester without your help. It's the least I can do to thank you."

"I'm just doing my job," I said. "You don't have to thank me."

"I *want* to thank you," she said. "And I know sororities are expensive, but we have payment plans. And financial aid. I'm happy to chat more about the details at the party."

She seemed strangely genuine.

But it didn't add up with what Lara had heard in the library yesterday.

Unless Courtney had approached Trent about it, and he'd assured her that nothing was going on between us?

That had to be it. It was the only thing that made sense.

And as crazy as it was, there was a part of me that wanted to consider it. No one had ever come this far out of their way to invite me to anything.

It felt surprisingly good.

Not like I could actually do it. I had enough on my plate with balancing school and my part-time job at the coffee shop.

I couldn't risk my grades.

Despite the little temptation I felt to go and check it out, I had to say no.

"I appreciate the offer," I said. "But I'm not sure I have the time for it right now."

"That's a shame." She frowned. "Joining a sorority

gives you amazing connections. The sort of connections that help you get fantastic job offers after graduation."

"Really?"

"Yep! I'm sure the girls would love to tell you more over dinner. We'll have free pizza. It'll be fun!"

She elongated the word "fun" so much that it sounded like she was begging me to come.

"And you know what our philanthropy is, right?" she continued.

"I didn't even know that sororities did charity work," I said honestly.

"It's called 'Help Children Read.'" She smiled again and squared her shoulders with pride. "We help get books into classrooms with students in need."

All right. Another point in Kappa's favor.

She reached for the strap of her bag, watching me expectantly as she waited for an answer.

Maybe it wouldn't hurt to give it a shot. It wasn't like I was going to sign my life away to them on the spot.

It was one party.

Totally do-able. And if it was awful, I could always leave.

"I'd have to get someone to cover my shift at work," I said slowly, shocked at myself for even considering this —and still shocked that she'd invited me. "If I can, I'll be there."

"Great!" She jumped slightly and clapped her hands together. "It's at 6:30, at the Kappa house. See you there!'

She spun around and pranced out of the room, and I stared after her, wondering what exactly I'd gotten myself into.

CHAPTER THREE

I 'd told myself that if the first person I called to cover my shift could do it, then it was meant to be that I attended the sorority bid party.

If she couldn't do it, then I wasn't meant to go.

I'd called my most unreliable co-worker.

By some miracle, she happily volunteered to cover my shift.

So, sorority party it was.

Which was why I was now sitting on a couch in the middle of a fancy common room, slowly eating a slice of pizza as three girls dressed in nearly identical sundresses hovered around me like vultures.

Courtney, Lacey, and another girl whose name started with a C.

Carrie? Or maybe Cara. One of the two.

"So," Carrie/Cara said. "What did you do over

winter break?" She sat forward eagerly, awaiting my response.

"Worked more shifts at the coffee shop," I said. "And caught up on some books by my favorite authors, since it's hard to get reading in for fun when we're in school."

She stared at me blankly.

"Cool," she said after a few seconds, although by the way she sat back into the couch, it was clear she thought it was anything but cool.

"What are you doing for spring break?" Lacey asked.

"I don't know." I shrugged. "Probably the same thing?"

"You mean you don't go skiing out west, or to Europe, or anything?"

"I've never left Florida," I said simply.

Lacey gave Courtney a *look*, as if she were trying to telepathically ask her for help—or to ask her what I was doing there.

I should have known better than to think I'd fit in at a sorority party.

It was becoming clearer by the minute that Courtney had only invited me because she felt like I was a charity case who deserved a reward for helping her boyfriend graduate college. She'd basically said as much when she'd asked me to come. I didn't know why I'd chosen to ignore it.

Future job connections, I reminded myself, although

the girls seemed more focused on where they liked to vacation than on their career aspirations.

I placed my slice of pizza down on my plate, about to tell them that I had to go home and study. After all, I *did* have that test tomorrow, even though I had more than enough time tonight to get ready for it. I'd never needed a lot of sleep, which came in handy in college.

Courtney slammed her drink down onto the coffee table, and the two other girls straightened. "How about we give you the house tour?" she asked brightly. "We'll explain our philanthropy as we walk."

"Sure," I said, grateful for her change of subject, especially since that *was* one of the things I'd been interested in learning about.

It couldn't hurt to hear her out.

She stood up and straightened imaginary creases out of her dress, like a future Stepford Wife. "Lacey. Carrie," she said to the two other girls. "Come with us."

Carrie. I was right on her name the first time.

Courtney led the way through the common room, past sorority girls who were "interviewing" the two other girls who'd been invited to the party.

As we passed, I heard one girl talking about a trip to Greece she'd taken with her family over winter break, and how cool it had been to see the Parthenon in person.

Seeing Grecian ruins *did* sound super interesting. I'd always thought it was incredible that we had such intact remains from a brilliantly advanced (for their time) society that had existed thousands of years ago.

I wanted to jump into the conversation, but someone pulled at my hand—Courtney—and directed me out of the common room. The hall lined with doors was far less fancy—it looked like a regular dorm.

"Let's not bother with the other rooms," she said. "Mine's the best." She strutted down the hall and stopped at the last door on the left. "It used to be a double," she explained. "But the fire department decided it was too small for two people, so now it's all mine."

She opened the door and motioned for me to come inside.

I widened my eyes when I walked in. Because I'd been in some of the dorm rooms on campus, but they were nothing like *this*.

Courtney didn't have the standard twin bed given to the on-campus students. She had a full-sized bed, with light green bedding that looked like it was made of silk. The desk had been replaced with what must have been a seventy-inch television. She also had two closets—presumably because the room had originally been for two people—and an expensive-looking full length mirror.

Goosebumps prickled along my arms, and I was suddenly aware of how much I was being watched.

"Close the door," Courtney commanded Lacey.

Lacey didn't just close the door—she dead-bolted it.

An unsettled feeling rose inside me.

I turned back around to look at Courtney, and her eyes were filled with anger so hot I swore I could feel it.

This was *not* the same friendly girl who'd pranced into the lounge earlier today and invited me to this party.

"I think I should go." I backed toward the door, but Lacey and Carrie were standing in front of it, blocking my only exit.

"You're not leaving until you admit the truth," Courtney sneered, the former perkiness in her tone replaced by animalistic hate.

"I don't know what you're talking about."

She took a threatening step toward me, and I backed up again on instinct. "Trent's been acting distant lately," she said. "So I thought: who at this school could pull his attention away from me? Then you came to mind—the aloof girl who tutors him in English."

"I didn't think you knew I existed before today." I held my gaze with hers, not wanting her to think she intimidated me.

At the same time, I was mentally prepping to defend myself in case she tried to claw my eyes out.

"Don't play dumb. *Everyone* knows you exist," she said hatefully. "Guys practically drool over you when you walk by, like you're some sort of goddess. And you don't even have to try." She looked me up and down, clearly judging my ripped black jeans and faded Hogwarts t-shirt.

"I'm not *playing* at anything," I said. "There's nothing going on between me and Trent."

"He talks about you, you know," she continued, as if she hadn't heard me. "He's amazed by how smart and helpful you are. And he's never cared about stuff like that. It's like you've cast some kind of spell on him."

I couldn't help it—I chuckled. "If I could cast love spells on people, Trent's the last person I'd choose."

Her eyes narrowed further. "Denying it isn't going to get you anywhere," she said. "Slut."

Anger heated inside me until my blood felt like it was boiling, and that low hum I'd felt last night during the Northern Lights vibrated through me.

The next thing I knew, Courtney reached into a display bowl on the end table next to her bed, picked up a handful of tiny decorative gems, and threw them at me.

I spun around and held my hands up to protect myself, readying myself for the impact.

Nothing hit me.

Instead, the gems did a one-eighty and turned themselves back at Courtney, flying at her with the same force she'd thrown them at me.

Her mouth dropped open, and she stumbled backward, tripping on her own feet and falling back into the wall. Her head smacked against the concrete, and she slumped down to her side, not moving.

The gems were splayed out on the floor around her.

I stood there in shock, and panic rushed through me. Because what I'd just seen was impossible. And Courtney still wasn't moving.

Lacey and Carrie ran to her side, and I took a few steps backward, unable to look away.

Did she hit her head hard enough to kill her?

No, she couldn't have.

But she still wasn't getting up.

Did I do that to her?

No. I didn't touch her. She'd tripped. It wasn't my fault.

But the way those gems had turned around and flown at her...

It wasn't possible. There had to be a logical explanation.

And she couldn't be dead. Her face was scratched up from the gems, but there wasn't a pool of blood beneath her head. She was just unconscious. She *had* to be.

Lacey was already on her phone calling for help.

Carrie looked over her shoulder and sneered at me, looking even more vicious than Courtney had moments before. "Get out of here," she said. *"Freak."*

I held my hands up like a bank robber caught by the police. "I didn't do anything," I said.

I didn't know who I was trying to convince—her, or me.

"Get. Out." She literally bared her teeth, like she was getting ready to attack.

Courtney still wasn't moving.

I studied my hands, not sure *what* I'd done to her, or if I'd even done it at all.

But Carrie still looked like she was about to pounce. And as much as I disliked her, I didn't want to accidentally hurt her, too.

So I spun around, hurried toward the door, and ran out of there without looking back.

CHAPTER FOUR

The drive home passed in a blur.

When I got back to the apartment, I slammed the door shut and ran to Lara's room.

She wasn't there.

But I'd seen her car next to mine in the parking lot. So I hurried back into the living room and opened the door to the balcony.

Lara was sitting on a chair with a textbook on her lap, a highlighter in her hand, and a half-finished glass of wine on the table next to her.

She snapped her head up to look at me.

"What happened?" she asked.

"I think I might have killed Courtney." The words came out of my mouth in a rush.

Lara placed the book down on her lap. "What are you talking about?"

"She didn't actually invite me there to see if I wanted to join the sorority. She brought me to her room, and she called me a slut because she thought I was hooking up with Trent, and then she picked up these little crystal-gem things and threw them at me, but I was so angry, and they turned back around to fly at her, and then she tripped backward and her head smacked into the wall..."

I paused to take a breath. The wind chimes rang behind me, like they were playing background music to my totally crazy story.

Lara was looking at me like I'd lost my mind. "I'm sure she's okay," she said, even though she had no way to actually know that.

"I don't know," I said. "She was so *still.*"

"But you didn't touch her. She tripped."

I nodded, replaying the scene in my mind for the hundredth time. I definitely hadn't touched her. "But those gems..." I said, since I couldn't make any sense of it.

"Are you sure she threw them at you?" Lara asked.

"Yes. I'm sure."

"And then they *spun back around* and hit her?"

"It sounds crazy," I said, since I didn't believe it myself. "But I know what I saw."

She nodded slowly, and I could tell she was at a loss for words.

I just stood there, trying to steady my breathing.

Had Courtney been breathing after she fell?

I didn't know. I hadn't looked.

I should have looked.

"Maybe it has to do with the magnetic field," Lara said, interrupting my train of thought. "The Northern Lights last night might have something to do with it. That's one of the theories online—that they appeared because of a shift in Earth's poles."

"What does that have to do with gems?" I asked.

"Gems are from the Earth?" she said. "I'm just theorizing here."

"Okay." I ran my fingers through my hair and took another deep breath. "You're right. Maybe that's it."

"Sit down," she said, and she picked up her phone. "I'll look it up."

I sat, but bounced my knee up and down, unable to sit still.

Lara was tapping on her phone, and from the intense way she was studying it, I could tell she wasn't finding much.

"Well?" I asked, unable to take the waiting.

"Hold on," she said, and I sat back in the chair, gazing out into the parking lot.

The more times I replayed the scene in Courtney's room in my head, the more times I wondered if I was remembering it correctly.

As I was thinking, a black SUV that was *definitely* too

fancy for this neighborhood turned into the parking lot and pulled into a space.

My heart rose into my throat.

Was it the cops? Did they track me here to question me? Or to bring me into the station?

"Let's go inside," I said to Lara, even though being inside wouldn't hide us from the cops.

Plus, I hadn't done anything wrong. I hadn't touched Courtney.

Still, I paced anxiously around the living room anyway.

Lara finished off the rest of her wine in a few seconds and kept scrolling through her phone.

I took my phone out to try to help, but my body was shaking so much that my fingers kept landing on the wrong keys. So I gave up, shoved my phone into the back pocket of my jeans, and kept pacing.

A knock on the door made me freeze in place.

"I'll get it," Lara said, and she jumped off the couch. "Stay here."

As if I had anywhere else to go? We were on the third floor, so I couldn't exactly jump off the balcony. Besides, I wasn't stupid enough to run from the cops. It would only make me look guilty.

I *wasn't* guilty. I knew that. I hadn't touched her.

But I felt like I was.

Lara opened the door, and I held my breath, panic rising in my chest.

Two people around our age stood on the other side. A girl with light blond hair, and a guy with dark hair. They both wore jeans, and she wore a white top, while his was deep red. Plus, they had backpacks, like they'd just come from the library.

"You don't look like the cops," I said, and the girl smiled slightly, her bright gray eyes twinkling with amusement.

"That's because we're not cops," she said. "Not anywhere *close* to it."

"Can we come in?" the guy asked.

Lara glanced at me, waiting for me to make the call.

Something inside of me—a something that could have been incredibly stupid—made me want to trust them.

"If you're not the cops, then who are you?" I asked, since either way, their arrival was beyond strange.

"I'm Nicole," she said, and she pointed to her companion. "This is Blake. We sensed a magical awakening in the area, so we came to check it out. We traced it here—to you."

A *magical awakening?*

"What?" I asked, totally dumbfounded.

"Last night, you discovered your magic," she replied.

"Our radar sensed it in this general area. Tonight, you used it on that girl on campus."

"You mean Courtney?"

I was barely processing what she was saying. Because it was crazy. Totally and completely crazy.

Then again...

I glanced down at my hand, since no matter how insane it sounded, I could have sworn I'd done something to those gems.

Lara stepped to my side. "Is this some kind of prank?" she asked them.

"Not a prank," Nicole continued, remaining focused on me. "You used a pretty large blast of magic. We went to the sorority house to check out what had happened, and it was a total commotion, but we managed to learn that you knocked that girl out and ran."

Relief released inside of me. "You mean she's not dead?"

"She'll have a nasty bruise," Nicole said. "And maybe a concussion. But she was very much alive. And she was convinced you used some sort of devil's sorcery to throw a bunch of crystals at her."

"She threw them at me," I said. "And then..." I trailed off, unsure how to explain it in a way that made sense.

"We're here to help you," the guy—Blake—said calmly, his tone reassuring.

Nicole was looking at me with so much hope.

"Are you like me?" I asked, even though I didn't know what *I* was. All I knew was that I needed help, or guidance, or something.

Not even my mom's midnight, incense-enhanced yoga sessions could prepare me for *this*.

"We are," she said. "If you let us in, we can explain more. Because like Blake said, we want to help you."

I looked to Lara, and this time, she shrugged.

Nicole and Blake watched me patiently.

I wanted to believe they were telling me the truth. But given what had happened with Courtney, I was beginning to think my truth-radar wasn't in tune today.

Maybe they were here because I was dangerous and they wanted to lock me in some sort of magical prison?

But they were my only leads on what had happened tonight. And they sounded sincere. If I sent them away, I'd regret it forever.

"I guess I have nothing to lose at this point," I said, and then I walked to the door, opened it further, and invited them in.

CHAPTER FIVE

The two of them walked awkwardly into the living room. Blake looked around, and he seemed less than impressed.

True, the apartment wasn't much. But what did he expect from two college freshmen?

I guessed a lot, given the luxury SUV they'd pulled up in.

"Any chance we can have something to drink?" Nicole asked. "We've been driving for hours."

"Sure," I said, glad that she didn't appear to be judging our apartment, too. "What do you want?"

"Water's fine," she said, and Blake agreed.

"Screw that," Lara said. "I'm getting my wine."

She brought both the bottle and her half-finished glass to the table, set them down, then walked to the fridge in our tiny kitchen to help me get the waters.

"You don't think they're serious, do you?" she whispered as she started filling the first glass with ice.

"I don't know." I shrugged. "But we might as well hear them out."

"Fine," she said. "But if they're pulling a prank on you like that sorority bitch..." Her eyes narrowed, like she was ready for a fight.

"I don't think they're pulling a prank," I said.

"Why not?"

"I just don't."

I'd say it was gut instinct, but the truth was, I didn't *want* this to be a prank.

I needed an explanation for what had happened back there. And what Nicole and Blake were saying made more sense than anything I'd come up with so far.

Lara didn't look convinced. But she helped me serve the drinks anyway, and we got situated around the small, round kitchen table that could barely fit four chairs around it.

Nicole and Blake had already settled in, their bags on the floor next to their feet.

I took a sip of my water and looked to Nicole, since she was by far the friendlier of the two. "All right," I said. "Explain."

"There's no easy way to say this, so I'm just gonna be out with it," she said. "We're witches. You are, too. And Blake and I are recruiters for Elementals Academy—a school that teaches the most powerful witches in the country how to use magic."

"You can't be serious," I said, even though they looked deadly so. "Witches don't exist."

Despite how new-agey my mom was, even she didn't believe in actual witches.

"It's easier if we show you," Blake said, and then he opened his hand, and a small ball of fire appeared in his palm.

It was about the size of a tennis ball, and I stared at it in shock as the flames danced around each other.

The fire could be an illusion. But I could feel the warmth of it radiating against my skin. And Blake's hand wasn't burning.

"How are you doing that?" I asked.

"I told you." He smirked. "Magic."

"Elementals Academy is a school for witches with elemental magic," Nicole said simply. "Earth, fire, wind, water, and spirit. As you can see, Blake's elemental affinity is fire."

"What's yours?" I asked.

"Spirit," she said, and then she reached for Blake's fire, and the flames consumed her hand.

Her face scrunched with pain as her skin blistered in the furnace of orange flame.

I could smell it cooking.

"Stop." I reached for my glass and splashed the water onto Blake's hand to put out the fire.

The fire went out, although not as instantly as I'd expect. It made me wonder if the water had actually done anything, or if Blake had chosen to put the fire out himself.

Nicole's hand was as grotesquely burned as you'd expect after being in an open flame for a few seconds.

My stomach churned as I stared at it.

"Relax," she said, although from the way her breaths were coming faster and a few beads of sweat had formed on her brow, she was clearly in pain.

Then she held her healthy hand over the burned one, and the skin healed in front of my eyes.

In seconds, it was as good as new.

She held it out for me to look at. "See?" she said proudly. "I'm fine."

"You can heal yourself," I said, even though it was obvious after what I'd just seen.

"And others."

I took a breath to try to compose myself, then looked at Lara.

She was staring at Nicole's hand, and she was abnormally quiet. Maybe she was in shock.

I turned back to face Nicole. "Did you have to show us like *that?*" I asked. "Couldn't you just have scratched yourself or something?"

"I've found that people accept the truth easier when I make it extra dramatic," she said simply.

She had a good point. Because after what I'd just seen, I knew they were telling the truth.

They could use magic.

They were *witches.*

And they'd come here for me.

"How long have you been doing this?" I asked, since I wasn't going anywhere with them unless I had answers.

"Six years," she said.

I sized her up. "How old are you?"

"Twenty-one."

She was two years older than me. I wasn't surprised, but that meant…

"You've been doing this since you were fifteen," I said.

"Yep," she said. "But that's a story for another time. Because right now, we're here to help *you.*"

"Because you think I have magic, too."

"We don't *think* you have magic," Blake said. "Given what those girls said happened at that sorority house, we *know* you have magic."

I glanced at Lara to see her reaction, and she yawned.

The lack of sleep from staying up last night must have been catching up with her. It probably wasn't helping that she was also drinking wine.

"Is that why the Northern Lights appeared last night?" I asked. "Was it magic?"

"We don't know any more about that than you do," she said. "But it's not abnormal for cosmic events to be connected to magic. The Elders are looking into it."

"Who are the Elders?" I asked.

"More experienced witches," she said, and I nodded, since that much was obvious from their name.

"Anyway," Blake said. "We're not here to talk about last night. We're here for you—because of what you did in that sorority house."

"I made those gems turn back around and smack into Courtney," I said, and this time when I said it, I knew it was true. "But *how?*"

"Probably air magic," Nicole said. "Air elementals can use their magic to make things fly. When they're super powerful, they can make huge things fly—even motor vehicles." Her eyes turned sad, and she glanced down at her lap. When she returned her gaze to mine, she was as composed as ever. "Most air elementals can't do anything that intense. But gemstones? Totally possible."

"I didn't mean to do it," I said, remembering the terrified look on Courtney's face when those gems came flying at her. "It just *happened.*"

"Which brings us back to why we're here," Blake

said. "Come with us to Elementals Academy, and you'll learn how to control your magic."

"And if I don't go?" I asked, since it didn't sound like they were giving me an option.

"Now that your magic has emerged, there are creatures out there who will be able to sense it. Sort of like how we just did," he said. "Monsters. They don't bother tracking regular witches, because they don't see them as a threat. Elemental witches, on the other hand…" He trailed off, letting me come to the conclusion myself.

These monsters would want me dead.

"What types of monsters?" I asked.

Nicole and Blake shared a *look*—the kind of look that can only be shared by two people who'd known each other for years. Like they were having a conversation with each other just by looking into each other's eyes.

In that moment, the strength of the bond between them became obvious. They loved each other—deeply.

Lara was surprisingly quiet. Another glance at her showed that her eyes were bloodshot.

Staying up so late last night was definitely getting to her.

"These monsters are ones from myth," Nicole said. "And trust me—you don't want to face them with untrained magic."

"Which is why you need to come with us to the academy, where you'll be trained and protected," Blake said.

"And if I don't?"

"Then whatever happens to you from here out is on you."

So, go with them to this mysterious academy, or get hunted by ancient monsters that would most likely kill me.

There wasn't much of a choice here.

"What should I tell my mom?" I asked. "And my teachers? And friends?"

Well, the few friends I had. Which were pretty much the ones from book club. They were more like acquaintances than anything else, but I'd like to think they'd notice if I suddenly disappeared.

"Don't worry," Nicole said. "This is far from the first time we've done this. The Elders know how to handle it. They'll make it so everyone close to you isn't worried about where you are. They'll think you transferred to a school in another state or something."

"So you want me to go with you and leave my entire life behind."

"Pretty much," Blake said.

"It won't be that bad," Nicole said quickly. "The academy isn't in another realm or anything. We have internet, and technology, and everything else you're used to here."

I glanced at my phone in relief, since I couldn't imagine a world without it.

Suddenly, Lara laid her arms down on the table, rested her head on them, and fell asleep.

I sat back in shock.

Because yes, we'd pulled an all-nighter. But this was hardly the type of conversation that would put someone to sleep.

Something was wrong.

I reached for her shoulder to wake her up. "Lara?" I said, shaking her again.

She didn't move.

My gaze immediately went to Blake's. "What did you do to her?"

"She saw too much," he said simply.

"We just put a little lotus juice in her wine," Nicole finished for him. "Don't worry—it's harmless. When she wakes up, she'll think this was all a dream. The Elders will take care of it from there."

"You mean you drugged her."

"It's better if she knows nothing," Blake said. "It's for her own good. Trust us."

"You just *drugged* my best friend." I glanced at Lara again in complete and utter shock. She was as passed out as someone would be after drinking a bottle of vodka.

"We did," Nicole said. "But you saw what we did with our magic. If we didn't want her to talk, why would we drug her when we could easily kill her?"

"I don't know." I shrugged, definitely relieved they

hadn't chosen that path. "But that doesn't make it okay that you drugged her."

"We're here for you—not her," Blake said simply, and I glared at him for talking about my best friend like she didn't matter at all.

"Lara's going to be okay," Nicole repeated. "But Blake's right—you're the one we're here for. Come with us to the academy and see it for yourself. If you don't like it, you're always free to leave."

"Then what? Be hunted by those monsters you told me about?"

"Yes," Blake said.

His bluntness took me by surprise.

"The academy isn't a prison," Nicole said. "But we've given you your choices. What you do from here is up to you."

She sat back and watched me, waiting for my decision.

I was pretty sure I knew what that decision would be.

But before I could reply, someone kicked the door open, knocking it off its hinges like in one of those cop shows.

Except it wasn't a some*one*.

It was a some*thing*.

I looked it up and down in shock.

No way was it real.

It might have passed as a woman, if not for the birdlike talons she had instead of feet, and the wings growing out of her arms. She stared at me with glowing yellow eyes, opened her mouth, and hissed, revealing long, sharp, deadly teeth.

I screamed, shot out of the chair, and backed into the kitchen, searching for an exit even though the only way out was the door the creature was standing in front of.

The bird-monster started running toward me.

My heart stopped, and I froze. I was going to become a meal for a monster before I could even get to the academy.

But a flaming arrow whizzed through the air and sank into the monster's chest.

It stopped moving, its eyes went wide, and it flickered a few times and disappeared.

The only thing that remained was its toga-like outfit on the floor.

I gripped the counter behind me as I caught my breath, my mind scrambling to make sense of what had just happened—even though it was what Nicole and Blake had just been telling me about.

Nicole stood next to the table, holding a bow with another arrow in it. Her backpack next to her feet was wide open.

Lara was still passed out, but thankfully, unharmed.

"Like we warned you," Nicole said, relaxing her hold on the bow. "You might have been able to fight off that catty sorority girl, but real monsters are an entirely different story."

"You did what most newbies do," Blake added. "You froze up."

I stared at the toga on the floor again and blinked a few times.

A few more seconds, and that thing would have ripped me to shreds.

"What. Was. That?" I finally said.

Nicole folded her bow, put it and the arrow into her backpack, and zipped it up. "That was a harpy," she said. "I *hate* harpies."

"You've seen one before?"

"A harpy was one of the first monsters I killed."

"How did it find us?"

"Simple," Blake said. "It sensed your magic."

"But you guys used magic, too," I said. "So it's not totally my fault."

"Your magic's untrained," he said. "It's like a beacon broadcasting your location to every monster in proximity. We have better control over our magic than that."

"The sort of control you can learn to have at Elementals Academy," Nicole chimed in.

She and Blake were silent, waiting for me to respond.

I glanced over at Lara again, who was still sleeping soundly, and all of it started to sink in.

If I didn't go to the academy, I wouldn't just be

putting myself in danger. I'd be putting the people around me in danger, too.

My friends and family could die because of me.

No way was I letting that happen.

I turned my focus back to Nicole and Blake with what I hoped was determination in my eyes. "When do we leave?" I asked.

Blake smirked, like he'd known what I was going to say before I'd said it.

"Pack a bag, and do it quickly," he said. "Because we're leaving now."

CHAPTER SIX

Once my bag was packed, we carried Lara to her bed, and Nicole and Blake walked me to their huge black Escalade. My eyes darted around the parking lot, on the lookout for more monsters, but all was still.

"How far is the academy?" I asked.

"It's about a twelve-hour drive," Nicole said.

I stopped walking the moment she said it.

"What?" she asked. "Do you get carsick or something?"

"No. It's just that I've never been out of Florida."

"Well, that's about to change," she said. "Because Elementals Academy is in Alexandria, Virginia."

"Wow," I said, because while that was far from the craziest thing that had happened in the past few hours, it still felt pretty huge. "Okay. Cool."

I tried to stay calm, despite the fact that driving to another state—and one so far away—felt surreal.

All of this felt surreal.

I followed them in a daze. Once we got to the car, Nicole threw my pack into the trunk, and Blake opened the door to the backseat for me.

The inside of the car was *massive,* and the leather looked and smelled brand new. I shifted uncomfortably as I pulled the seatbelt over my chest and snapped it in place.

Blake hopped into the driver's seat, and Nicole sat shotgun.

"You should try to sleep," Blake said to me once we were settled in. "It'll be morning when we get there."

"I just used magic I didn't know I had, thought I'd killed Courtney, and was almost killed by a monster that until today, I didn't think existed," I said. "*And* we're on our way to the real life equivalent of Hogwarts. How am I supposed to sleep after all of that?"

"You just used your magic for the first time—and a pretty large amount of it, at that," Nicole said. "You'll be able to sleep."

I didn't believe her.

But my eyes felt heavy by the time we turned onto the main road, and I was totally out before we even hit the highway.

I woke to a slice of sunlight peeking through the window. We were still driving, and my arm had pins and needles from sleeping the wrong way.

I rubbed the sleep out of my eyes and shook out my arm.

Nicole looked back at me and smiled. "You're up," she said. "Good timing. We're almost to the academy."

"What time is it?" I asked.

"Seven AM."

I did the quick calculation in my mind. "Are you saying I slept for ten hours?"

"Yep," she said. "You were totally out."

"That's not possible," I said, but then I remembered Lara falling asleep on the table. "Did you sneak me some of that drug, too?"

"No," she said. "I promise."

I glanced away for a second, since I technically had no reason to trust this girl I'd met less than a day ago.

Minus the fact that she'd saved my life.

"She's telling the truth," Blake said. "You haven't drank anything since before the harpy attacked. Even if we wanted to drug you, we wouldn't have had a chance."

"True," I said, since he had a point. "It's just that I've never slept that long in my entire life."

Nicole raised an eyebrow. "Seriously?"

"I don't need a lot of sleep." I shrugged. "From your reaction, I guess that's not a witch thing."

"Definitely not a witch thing," she said. "I *love* my sleep."

I nodded, then looked out the window, surprised to see actual hills.

Everything in Florida was flat. I'd seen hills on tv before, but they looked far more expansive in real life. It was also gray outside. Really, really gray. A thick sheet of clouds covered the sky, making the world look undersaturated and dull. And the huge, wide trees looked dead, with no leaves on their bare, brown branches.

"Welcome to Virginia," Nicole said brightly. "What do you think?"

"It's kind of depressing."

Really depressing.

"Tell me about it," she said. "I grew up in Georgia and moved up north when I was fifteen. I hated it."

"She still hates it," Blake said.

"I hate the winter. And the fall. And early spring," she said. "But don't worry—it gets better in the summer when the sun's out."

"Which won't matter, since we won't be in school," I pointed out.

"About that," Nicole said slowly. "Elementals Academy is a year-round school."

I did a double-take, since I didn't even know that was a thing.

"We have breaks," she added, apparently sensing my alarm. "But you'll have to wait to go home until you have better control over your magic. Well, we recommend waiting. Whatever you choose to do is up to you."

I nodded, since I had zero desire to be around anyone until I had better control over my magic. I also had no idea what I'd say to people to explain why I'd left. Nicole had said the Elders would "handle it," but what did that even mean?

"The school is right around this hill," Blake said, and I sat more alert, ready to see the academy.

Turned out there wasn't much to see yet. Only a tall, cement block fence with red tiled roofs poking out above it. There was a single opening in the protective wall—a columned arch that reminded me of the Arc de Triomphe. The words carved into the top of the arch read *The Emerson-Abbot Academy.*

"I thought it was called Elementals Academy?" I asked.

"That's what everyone calls it," Nicole said. "But it's not the school's official name."

"Got it," I said, since Elementals Academy *did* flow a lot better.

Blake drove through the arch and entered a campus that looked like it had come straight out of the Mediterranean. It was prettier than any college campus I'd ever seen in my life. It looked like what I imagined the Grecian ruins must have looked like back in their heyday.

Eventually, he pulled into a spot near a huge lawn in front of one of the larger buildings. Both of them hopped out of the car, and Nicole opened the door for me.

Freezing cold air blew its way inside, hitting me like a thousand needles at once.

I gasped, sat back, and rubbed my hands over my arms.

Blake removed his leather jacket and handed it to me. "Put this on," he said.

He only wore a t-shirt underneath, but his bare arms didn't even have goosebumps on them.

"Won't you be cold?" I asked as I put on his jacket, which was better, but not totally.

It probably also didn't help that I was wearing flip-flops.

"My element is fire." He created a small fireball in his palm—as if I could forget his ability—then snuffed it out. "I don't get cold."

"Oh," I said. "Lucky."

"Right?" Nicole said. "It's not fair. But air students can sometimes warm up or cool down the air around them. It's a higher-level ability, but judging by how much magic you used on your first try, I have a feeling you'll get there."

"Thanks," I said, and just for the hell of it, I wished for the air around me to warm up.

Nothing happened.

Unsurprising, given what Nicole had just told me.

"Come on," she said. "The main building is the big one across the field. Our headmistress is excited to meet you."

There were students walking around campus, likely heading to their next class. They all looked so normal—I would have had no idea they were actual witches if I'd passed them on the street. Although as a whole, they were more attractive than what you'd see around a regular college campus. It was like we were walking through the set of a Hollywood studio.

We were halfway there when my eyes locked with the ice-blue ones of an insanely gorgeous guy ahead. With his jet-black hair and pale skin, he was unnaturally striking—like a porcelain god. I would have thought he was a supernatural even before I knew witches existed.

The way he was looking at me made me feel like he was seeing into my soul.

He blinked a few times, shook his head slightly, and glanced away, as if he was coming out of a trance. The air chilled as he walked by, and I wrapped Blake's jacket tighter around myself to try to keep warm.

He didn't so much as glance at me again, and I did my best to continue as if the sight of him hadn't made me nearly stop in my tracks.

Finally, we reached the wide, marble steps of the main building and walked up to the entrance. It was lined with columns, and there were tall, double-doors to get inside. I felt like I was arriving at a massive Grecian temple.

"Welcome to Elementals Academy," Blake said, and then he opened the door, and I walked inside a building with tiled floors and a grand staircase fancier than anything I'd ever seen in a college in my life.

CHAPTER SEVEN

I followed them up the staircase, and Nicole paused in front of the first door at the top.

She knocked twice, and a teen girl with shiny auburn hair, bright green eyes, and a flawless complexion opened the door.

"You must be Summer Donovan," she said, and I nodded. "I'm Kate—the headmistress of the school. I've been looking forward to meeting you."

"*You're* the headmistress?" I couldn't keep the shock out of my voice.

"I know—I look young." She chuckled, then opened the door wider, revealing a huge office that seemed to have a plant or flower on every available surface. On the ones without greenery, there were books. "But as the goddess of demigods and witches in-training, I take my responsibility to make sure you're prepared to face anything out there in the real world very seriously."

"Wait." I stopped walking. "You're a *goddess?*"

"Take a seat, and I'll explain everything." She motioned to one of the comfy armchairs facing her desk, and I did as requested.

Nicole took the seat next to me, and Blake remained standing.

Kate sat across from me, and the more I looked at her, the more ethereal I realized she was. At the same time, she seemed so human. It was a strange combination.

"You already know you're a witch—specifically, an elemental witch," she started, and I nodded, even though none of this felt real. "Well, the magic in our blood comes from the gods. All witches have a godly ancestor somewhere in their bloodline."

I stared at her, shocked speechless, my head spinning as I repeated her last two sentences in my mind.

"You have questions," she said simply.

Understatement of the century.

I searched my mind for where to begin.

"You said gods, plural," I said, and she nodded. "What gods are you talking about?"

"The Greek gods," she said simply.

"You know—Zeus, Poseidon, Ares, and all of them," Nicole added.

"Yeah. I've heard of them." I paused and played with

the tips of my fingers as I tried to process this. "You're saying that the Greek gods hooked up with our ancestors thousands of years ago?"

It was a general guess based on how old the ruins in Greece were.

"It varies," Kate said. "Sometimes, yes. It can also be hundreds of years. Or, in rarer cases, the god could be one of your parents."

"Like me," Nicole said. "I'm a demigod. My bio-dad is Apollo."

She said it so calmly—like she was telling me that one of her parents was a friend of my mom's.

"Okay," I said, and I looked to Blake. "Are you a demigod, too?"

"I'm a witch," he said simply.

"One of the original elemental witches," Nicole added, as if that should mean something to me.

"Since magic passes through family bloodlines, most witches already know they're witches when they get their elemental magic," Kate continued. "Have your parents ever given you any clues about your magical heritage?"

"I'm adopted." I shrugged. "I was dropped off at the doorstep of the local church when I was a baby. My mom knows nothing about my birth parents."

Kate and Nicole gave each other a knowing look.

"What?" I asked.

"Adoption or a parent who's absent from their child's life are the most common reasons why a witch doesn't know about his or her magical heritage," Kate said.

"Is there any way we can find out who my Greek ancestor is?" I sat closer to the edge of my seat, since I'd always wanted to know about my heritage. It seemed surreal that I might be about to find out.

Nicole fiddled with the sun pendant on her necklace. "Eventually, your ancestor will leave you a token to claim you," she said. "Apollo left this on my windowsill about a week after I got my magic."

"The timeline varies," Kate jumped back in. "Some find out in a day. For others, it takes years. But we can narrow it down based on what type of elemental magic you have. From what Nicole told me during your car ride here, it seems like you're an air elemental. But we need to test your magic to make sure. It's how we decide which dorm to place you in."

"How do you 'test' my magic?" I asked.

She smiled knowingly. "Follow me, and I'll show you."

CHAPTER EIGHT

The testing room was down the hall. The only things inside it were a bookshelf full of display items, a table, and two chairs.

"Have a seat," Kate said. "I'll grab the materials."

I did as she said, watching as she brought over a red candle, a lighter, a potted bunch of roses whose petals were still buds, a bowl of water, and yellow crepe paper crumpled into a ball. Once all of them were on the table, she sat down in the chair across from me.

"We're going to test you for all five elements, but it makes the most sense to start with air." She pointed to the crumpled piece of yellow paper. "Try to use your magic to create a strong enough breeze to blow this off the table."

I focused on the paper and tried to will it to move with my mind.

"You need to use your hands," Kate said gently. "Our magic comes out of our palms."

"Okay." I raised my hands and faced my palms toward the paper. I felt ridiculous, but I took a deep breath and focused.

Nothing happened.

"Dig into your core," she instructed. "Think of the color yellow—it's the color associated with air. Pull the yellow energy up through your body, then direct it through your palms and toward the paper."

Okay. I could do that.

I pictured the color yellow in my mind and did as Kate instructed.

Again, the paper didn't move.

"Hm." She pursed her lips, unsatisfied. "Let's move onto something else." She eyed the other items on the table. Finally, she replaced the paper with the candle and lit it. "Focus on the fire, and red energy," she said. "Try to connect with the flame and make it rise."

I had a feeling this was going to go about as well as it had with the crepe paper.

As suspected, the flame did nothing. I couldn't even put it out by my supposed air magic.

Next, Kate put out the candle and replaced it with the bowl of water. This time I had to focus on the color blue and try to create a ripple in the water.

Nothing again.

Finally, she replaced the bowl of water with the potted rose buds. "Think of green and try to get the roses to bloom," she said.

I focused. Really, really hard.

Still, nothing happened.

Kate held her palm out to face the roses, and they bloomed into beautiful pink flowers.

"I take it you're an earth elemental," I said.

"The first one in thousands of years. Like how Blake is with fire, and Nicole is with spirit. Which brings us to the final element." She pricked the pad of her index finger on one of the rose's thorns, then held it out to me. A tiny bit of blood bubbled up onto the surface of her skin. "Think of the color white, touch my finger, and try to heal it."

"Why do I use touch with this one and not the others?"

"No idea," she said. "I suppose it's one of the many mysteries of the universe."

I cautiously pressed the pad of my index finger onto hers, unsure what it would feel like to touch a goddess. Surprisingly, it felt no different than touching a human.

I closed my eyes, focused on the color white, and imagined the prick on Kate's finger healing. I tried so hard to push white energy out of me and into her, although it didn't feel like anything was happening.

I opened my eyes and lifted my finger from Kate's. Sure enough, the prick was still there.

She stared at it, silent.

"That wasn't normal, was it?" I finally asked.

"Nicole is the only witch able to control spirit," she said. "And judging by your story of how your element emerged, I doubted you'd be able to use healing magic. But I had to try, just like I do with all new students."

"I meant that it wasn't normal for me to not be able to control *any* of the elements."

She took a slow, deep breath in. "Like I said, there are many mysteries of the universe," she said. "But I'm not going to lie to you. No elemental witch has ever come into their element and been unable to use at least a bit of it during this test."

"So I'm a freak."

No change from what I'd been used to for my entire life. But now that I was at a *school* for freaks, I'd hoped I'd finally fit in.

"You're not a freak," she said kindly. "There's a first time for everything. You might just need to grow into your magic."

"Unless you made a mistake, and what happened with Courtney wasn't magic," I said.

"I promise you it was magic." She gave me a reassuring smile. "Our magic detectors have never been wrong."

"Like you said—there's a first time for everything."

I didn't mean for it to come out sarcastic. But it did anyway.

"Sorry." I couldn't bring myself to meet her eyes. "This is just really frustrating."

"I know," she said. "But given what happened with Courtney, it sounds like your element is air. So I'm going to place you into the air dorm. Hopefully being surrounded by other air elementals will help you tap into your magic."

"Sure," I said, since I was highly skeptical. "Sounds good."

"I'll prepare your schedule over the weekend, so you'll be ready to start classes on Monday," she said. "You'll have a bunch to catch up on, but I know your teachers will be happy to help."

"Let me guess," I said. "Students don't come to the school mid-semester, either?"

"Minus the original elementals, the gods have always chosen to gift their descendants with elemental magic during one of our breaks," she said. "But you're only a week behind, so it shouldn't be an issue."

Yet another thing that made me different from the others at the academy.

I glanced at the yellow crepe paper again, faced my palm toward it, and tried to make it move.

Come on, I thought. *Do something.*

Kate watched me sadly.

She felt bad for me. Great. Just great.

"Hey," she said, and when I met her eyes, I could tell how much she wanted me to feel comfortable. "This is all going to work itself out. Now, how about you come with me to the air dorm, so I can show you to your new room?"

"Okay," I said, since what else was I going to do? Leave the school?

No.

So, to the air dorm it was.

CHAPTER NINE

Nicole was waiting for us outside the door of the testing room.

"So?" she asked excitedly. "How high did you make that paper fly?"

"I didn't," I said flatly.

"What?"

"I couldn't do anything to the paper."

She tilted her head, confused. "So you're another element?"

"No," I said. "I failed the test."

"You didn't fail the test," Kate broke in. "You just need more time to learn how to harness your magic."

Nicole looked at Kate in confusion, but Kate didn't acknowledge her.

Disappointment filled my chest—disappointment in

myself. Because I was a straight-A student. I'd never failed a test.

"Are you sure I belong here?" I finally asked. "I wasn't the only one in that room when the crystals flew. Maybe one of the others did it." I searched my mind quickly for Courtney's friends' names. "Lacey or Carrie."

But as I said it, I didn't believe it. Because when those crystals flew back, I'd *felt* something. A buzz of something.

Magic.

Too bad it chose to not make an appearance in that testing room.

"I'm sure," Nicole said. "Those girls were as human as could be. I could tell by the way they looked at me and Blake."

"What do you mean?"

"I mean that they were intimidated. Subservient. Most humans get that way around witches. Especially around demigods."

"Lara didn't," I pointed out.

"Who's Lara?" Kate asked.

"My best friend," I told her. "Pretty much my *only* friend."

She studied me for a moment, and understanding crossed her eyes. "It sounds like it's been hard for you to not know about your heritage," she said. "But I'm glad you had someone in your life as a support system. Not all lost witches do."

Lost witches.

That pretty much described the way I'd felt for my whole life.

"Me, too," I agreed, since I couldn't imagine how tough things would have been without Lara. "But what makes her different?"

"Occasionally, a human is stronger than others," she said. "We think they might have extremely diluted witch blood far back in their family line. Not enough to use any magic, but enough to be comfortable around us. It sounds like Lara is one of those people."

"I wasn't too focused on her in your apartment, since my assignment was to recruit you," Nicole said. "But yeah, I could see it." Then she turned to Kate. "Since we haven't determined Summer's element yet, should she stay with us?"

She looked excited—like she wanted me to stay wherever they lived.

Had I just made my first friend here?

"No," Kate said, and my heart dropped, even though Kate had already told me her plans for me. "Everything that happened with her points toward her being an air elemental. I want her to live in the air dorm for now, since being around other air elementals might help her harness her magic."

Nicole looked at me and shrugged, as if saying, *I tried.*

"Where do you guys live?" I asked.

"Kinsley Cottage," Nicole said. "It's near the middle of campus. Kate, Blake, and I—the three remaining original elementals—live there. It's hard to miss, since it's the only building on campus with wood sidings instead of concrete. If you need us, you can find us there. Or better yet…" She reached into her back pocket and pulled out her phone. "What's your number?"

I rattled it off quickly.

She typed it into her phone, pressed send, then smiled. "Just sent you a text. Now you have my number."

"Cool." I tried to return her smile, but I was pretty sure I looked awkward as hell. I'd never had anyone other than Lara actually *try* to be my friend. "Are you this nice to every new student?"

"I know what it's like to be new and thrown into a magical world I had no idea existed," she said. "I like to make sure people like us are comfortable. Plus, I was pretty amused when you tried to use your glass of water to put out Blake's fire."

"He was burning your hand," I said. "I had to do *something.*"

"And your natural instinct to take action is what's going to make you a great witch."

"Thanks." I stumbled over the word a bit, since after my awful performance on the magic test, a compliment was the last thing I'd expected.

Kate looked back and forth between us, although she made no move to share her number with me. It probably had something to do with her being a teacher and me being a student.

Or with her being a *goddess* and me being a witch.

"Now, how about I show you to your room so you can get settled in?" she asked.

"My stuff's in Blake's trunk," I said. "And it's only overnight stuff. I don't have anything else."

"Don't worry—all your stuff will be here by this evening," she said.

"Great." I figured they were getting my stuff by using some type of magic they didn't want to explain to me. The same magic they'd use so no one questioned why I'd transferred to a different school.

Secrets were starting to feel like a pattern around here.

Then I looked out the window at the blanket of gray clouds overhead, shivered at the thought of the cold waiting for us outside, and zipped Blake's jacket back up. I'd never had a leather jacket before, but I liked the feel of it. It suited me.

Nicole glanced down at my flip-flops. "I'm going to

guess that your collection of winter clothes is basically non-existent."

"I've never left Florida," I reminded her. "So, yeah. My 'winter clothes' are sweatshirts and sneakers."

"There's a great mall about twenty-five minutes from here," she said. "Tysons Corner. We can go tomorrow."

Numbers started whirring through my mind. "I probably have enough to get a winter jacket and boots," I said, trying to push down the panic that was definitely leaking into my tone. "Assuming it's an outlet mall?"

My voice went higher at the last part, because after a semester at Hollins, I knew what expensive clothes looked like—even the "casual expensive" kind of clothes, like designer jeans and jackets.

Judging by what Nicole and Kate were wearing, they didn't shop at outlet malls.

"Sorry—I think I got ahead of myself," Nicole said. "Everything you need will be paid for by the academy. It'll take a few days for your credit card to arrive, so we can just put everything on mine tomorrow."

"You're giving me a credit card?" I repeated, completely dumbfounded.

The only cards I'd ever had were my debit card (which currently had a frighteningly low balance on it) and my driver's license.

"Every new student gets one." She shrugged, like it was no big deal. "They're paid for by our benefactors, as is our tuition. They'll take care of any debt or loans you had before this, too."

Shock hit me like a truck. "They're going to pay off my student loans?" I asked. "Just like that?"

"Yep." She smiled. "Elemental witches and demigods keep the world safe from creatures like that harpy we met back in your apartment. Our benefactors understand how stressful debt can be, and they don't want us to worry about anything other than our training."

"The credit cards do have limits though," Kate broke in, like a concerned parent.

Then she told me the limit.

It was more than I made at the coffee shop in a *year*.

"You've gotta be kidding me," I said after the massive amount of shock started to set in.

Nicole smiled again. "You're more surprised by this than the fact that you're a witch."

"I had a partial scholarship for school *and* a part time job, and was still barely getting by," I explained. "That amount of money is unreal to me."

"Well, now it's real," Nicole said. "At least, it will be when you get your credit card."

I couldn't imagine what this credit card would look like.

It was probably made of solid gold.

"Anyway, I know Kate wants to walk you to your dorm," Nicole said, and the four of us headed down the steps. "Blake will bring your stuff over. I'll text you tomorrow and we can figure out when to go to the mall."

"Sure," I said, although I felt like I was living someone else's life instead of mine. "Talk tomorrow."

Kate glanced down at my naked toes. "We'll walk quickly," she promised, and then she pushed open the door, and we hurried out toward the dorm that was going to be my home for however long it would take me to learn to control my magic.

CHAPTER TEN

The paths were pretty empty as Kate and I hurried through campus. I assumed the students were all in classes.

"There are about two hundred students in the academy," Kate explained. "Spread pretty evenly across the four elements."

"Except for Nicole," I pointed out.

"Nicole is unique," Kate said. "Her father—Apollo—gifts his other descendants with air."

"So why did Nicole get spirit?"

"Long story short, the five original elementals were given our magic to complete an important task. For that task, one of us needed to control spirit. Now that the task is complete, no demigod or witch has been gifted with spirit. You'll learn more about it in your classes."

I nodded, since I had a feeling there was going to be a *lot* for me to catch up on in my classes.

"All students use smart watches as their key to access everything on campus," she continued. "You'll find yours in your room, along with a laptop, the latest model cell phone, and the books and materials you'll need for your classes."

"Wow," I said. "That was fast."

"We always keep two rooms in each dorm ready for potential new students. One for a female, and one for a male," she said. "Just in case."

"Just in case a freak incident occurs where a person receives their magic after the semester's already started?"

"Exactly."

Finally, Kate stopped in front of a large building about four stories tall. It was built in the Grecian style, like all the other buildings except Kinsley Cottage. Columns lined the entrance, and ΑΕΡΑΣ was carved in large letters on the plaque above the door.

"That's the Greek word for air," Kate explained, and she held her watch up to a scanner beside the door.

The door clicked open, and she led the way inside. The foyer had high ceilings and light wood floors—it was prettier than any dorm at Hollins. And that was saying something, since Hollins was one of the most beautiful colleges in America.

Off to the side was a common room that would put the Kappa house to shame. It was bright and airy, with large windows, comfy looking couches, and a large television. It looked like it belonged in a design magazine—not in a college.

"That's the common room," Kate said what I'd already realized, and then she opened the door at the other side of the hall to a room that looked like a cool, modern restaurant. "This is the dining room. A light breakfast and dinner is catered to each dorm, along with lunch on the weekends. Students are required to go to the main dining hall for lunch on weekdays, to socialize with students outside their element."

"Got it," I said, looking around the empty room. "I'm guessing everyone's in class?"

"Yep." She glanced at her watch. "Classes get out in about fifteen minutes. I wanted to get you inside the dorm before other students start filtering in, so you can meet your suitemate and get settled in peace. I messaged her professor and requested that he let her out of class early so she could return to the dorm as quickly as possible," she said, and then she turned to a circular staircase that looked like it belonged in a palace and led me up to the top floor.

The floor was smaller than the others. It felt like we'd gone to the top of a treehouse.

"Here it is." She held her watch up to the scanner on one of the wooden doors, and the lock clicked open.

"You can get into our rooms?" I asked.

"I'm the headmistress," she said. "My watch opens every lock in the academy. But don't worry—it's just a safety precaution. I've never entered a student's room without their permission."

"Cool," I said, since she seemed trustworthy.

She held open the door for me and I walked inside.

The room put Courtney's to shame. It was larger and way fancier—like I was in a luxury hotel instead of a college dorm. It had beautiful hardwood floors with a patterned gold rug in the center, a full-size bed, an elegant wooden wardrobe, a matching bookshelf that was already stocked with books, and a flat screen television attached to the wall across from the bed. The desk had three brand new boxes on it—a MacBook Pro, an Apple watch, and an iPhone.

There was also a door on the inside wall.

"Where does that go?" I asked Kate.

"The bathroom," she said. "Each suite has two rooms with a shared bathroom between them."

"Nice," I said, since it was an upgrade from the communal bathrooms in the dorms at Hollins. At the same time, I'd never had to share a bathroom, since the house I'd lived in with my mom and the apartment I'd shared with Lara each had two of them.

Hopefully my suitemate didn't like to hog the shower.

Kate had the door to my room propped open, and she was standing next to it. "A school-wide message of your arrival will be sent to the students and faculty in about ten minutes," she said.

"What?" My eyes must have been bulging out of my head. "Why?"

"As you know, a student has never started at the academy after the semester has begun. I can still stop the message from sending," she said. "But do you want everyone trying to figure out who you are and what you're doing here, or would you prefer that they're prepared?"

"Good point," I said, since I was going to be enough of a circus freak as it was.

At least this way, the student body would be aware that the circus was coming to town.

Then I heard someone coming up the stairs.

It had to be my suitemate.

Please be nice, I thought, since sharing a suite with someone like Courtney was one of my biggest fears.

It was possible that Courtney had been more monstrous than the harpy. Because unlike Courtney, the harpy hadn't attacked me on a personal level.

"Alyssa," Kate said warmly. "Come meet your new suitemate."

A short girl with wavy blond hair pranced inside, wearing a bright purple trench coat that flared at the bottom like a dress. She smiled widely when she saw me.

I groaned inwardly. She looked like she could be Courtney's sister.

"Hi!" she said. "I'm Alyssa. You're Summer, right? I heard you got your magic a little late. But that's okay. The air dorm is super fun and everyone's super nice. I'm sure you'll fit right in."

As she said the last part, she sounded a bit hesitant.

I didn't blame her. If everyone in this dorm was as bubbly as she was, I was going to stick out as much as I did at the sorority bid party.

She bounced on her toes, eyes wide as she waited for me to answer.

It's not her fault that she looks like Courtney, I told myself. *And I'm going to be practically living with her for the semester. Give her a chance.*

"Hi," I said. "I like your coat."

My mom always told me that if I didn't know what to say to someone, it never failed to give them a compliment.

"Thanks!" She beamed. "Purple's my favorite color. Obviously, since I'm a descendent of Dionysus. Do you know who your ancestor is yet?"

"No," I said. "Not yet."

"That's okay. Most people don't on their first day. I'm sure you'll find out soon."

"I hope so."

Kate looked back and forth between us, apparently satisfied by how the introduction went. "I'm going to leave you two to get acquainted," she said. "And Summer?"

"Yes?"

"You're with others like you now. I know it'll be a big adjustment, but the academy is your home. You're safe here."

"Thanks," I said, and then she closed the door, leaving me alone with Alyssa.

Alyssa took a deep breath and pulled her bag closer to her side. It was a designer bag similar to the ones the girls at Hollins wore. "So, this is your room," she said, gesturing around. "It'll look great once you decorate it and stuff."

As if it didn't look great now?

She walked to the other door, opened it, and led the way into the bathroom. Like the bedroom, it looked like it belonged in a luxury hotel.

And there was an explosion of girly products all over the marble countertop on both sides of the sink.

"Don't worry—I'll move that tonight," she said. "I'll take the right side and you can have the left. Sound good?"

"Great," I said, even though I had no idea how she was going to condense all of that to one side.

She walked to the other door and reached for the knob. "And this," she said with a flourish. "Is my room." She opened the door, revealing a room full of light purple and gold decorations. Everything that could be one of those colors—the comforter, curtains, rugs, and artwork—had been styled to fit the theme.

"Wow," I said. "You really do love purple."

"Yep!" she replied eagerly. "I can help you decorate your room. If you want."

"Sure." I didn't have the heart to tell her no.

I'd just have to make sure it didn't look like Barney had vomited all over my room.

"So," I said, looking around while searching for something to say. "Do we have pantries or kitchenettes or something?"

She looked at me like I'd asked her to paint my walls black.

"Of course not." She chuckled. "We eat all our meals downstairs or in the dining hall. There are always snacks down there, too. But I'll tell you what I *do* have." She paused dramatically, then walked to the other side of her desk and opened something up. "A mini-fridge! Do you want a drink? I have pinot noir, merlot, chianti—"

"It's barely lunchtime," I interrupted, and she froze,

apparently caught off-guard. "And don't you have classes in the afternoon?"

She straightened and smiled. "As a descendent of Dionysus, it's my job to make sure your first day here is *fun*," she said. "How about a mimosa? Mostly champagne, with just a drop of orange juice?"

"How about all orange juice and no champagne?" I asked with what I hoped was a friendly smile.

"Fine." She pouted, then took two clear plastic cups from the space next to the mini fridge. She poured our drinks and handed mine to me. "Cheers," she said. "To your first day at Elementals Academy."

"Thanks." I tapped her glass with mine, then took a sip. All orange juice. Not like I'd expected her to spike mine with champagne, but you never knew.

"Hey," she said, her tone more serious. "I know you're nervous about starting here after the semester's already begun. But I believe there's a reason the gods made us suitemates. I've got your back. I promise."

"I'm sure I'll be okay," I said, even though I definitely *wasn't* sure I'd be okay. "But I appreciate it. Truly."

"Anytime," she said. "Now—lunch is about to start. Let's go to the dining hall, and I'll introduce you to everyone?"

"Who's 'everyone'?" Horror traveled down my spine at the thought of her announcing my arrival to the entire dining hall.

"Just my group of friends." She took a second to eye me up. "That jacket doesn't look very warm. Do you need to borrow a coat? And boots?"

"I don't think we're the same shoe size," I said, since she was far more petite than me. Which was saying something, since I'd never considered myself to be tall. "But yeah—a jacket would be great."

And that was how I ended up in a bright purple coat, walking with Alyssa to face a bunch of witches and demigods in the dining hall of a magical academy.

CHAPTER ELEVEN

No one approached us as we walked to the dining hall, but they were definitely whispering to each other as we passed.

I tried my hardest to ignore them and focus on Alyssa's never-ending chitchat.

Finally, we reached the dining hall. It was multiple floors tall, with marble columns—which seemed to be on every building in the academy—and there was a bubbling fountain in front of it.

"This place is unreal," I told Alyssa.

"It's magical." She smiled. "I want to say you'll get used to it, but after being here for one semester, I'm still in awe whenever I walk around."

"If there's one thing I know I'll never get used to, it's how cold it is here," I said, since my toes were so numb by this point that I couldn't feel them.

"I'm from Massachusetts, and I'll never get used to it, either," she said, and we hurried up the steps, and she opened the doors for us to go inside.

The dining hall looked more like an upscale Greek tavern than a college cafeteria. Vines and leaves wrapped around the beams in the ceiling, and there were floor-to-ceiling windows that overlooked the lake behind the building.

The majority of students inside kept looking at us and cupping their hands around their faces as they spoke quietly to each other, as if we didn't know they were talking about us.

"I used to be frustrated at feeling like a ghost wherever I went," I said. "Apparently I didn't know how good I had it."

"Maybe they'll move onto something else soon," Alyssa said. "But it's a small school. It'll probably take a bit."

Great. Just great.

I scanned the groups sitting at the tables, and that was when I saw him.

The guy with jet black hair and ice-blue eyes who I'd crossed paths with that morning. He was sitting at a long table at the back, and he was staring at me with a cold, calculating gaze. Chills rushed up my spine, like he'd somehow touched me from across the room.

He quickly looked away and started talking to the

girl next to him. The tingles traveling through my body disappeared.

"Who's that guy at the table in the back?" I asked Alyssa as we walked to the food line.

"Which one?"

"Black hair. Pale skin. Ice-blue eyes."

She glanced over her shoulder. "You mean Zane Caldwell?"

"I don't know who I mean, since I don't know his name. But he's sitting next to the blonde who looks like a real-life Barbie."

Now that I thought about it, everyone at that table was completely stunning. Even more so than most of the others I'd seen around campus so far.

"Then you mean Zane," she said. "The girl next to him is Vera."

Jealousy that I shouldn't be feeling, given the fact that I'd never spoken to him in my life, zipped through me.

"They're not together," Alyssa said as we grabbed our trays. "In case you were wondering."

"I wasn't wondering."

"You were totally wondering. But I get it. He's hot. They all are."

"Who's 'they all'?" I asked, looking around at the food options. There seemed to be everything—salads, sandwiches, a variety of hot food, and even sushi.

"That table is full of descendants of Aphrodite," she

said. "The goddess of love. That's why they're insanely beautiful. They're also the biggest snobs at this school. Especially Zane. He's the iciest of them all—he even has ice magic to prove it. He hasn't actually been claimed by Aphrodite yet, but everyone assumes he's one of her descendants, given his looks and water magic."

"Oh," I said. "Interesting."

"He's never been interested in any of the girls at school," she continued. "But we have lots of hot guys in the air dorm. I'll introduce you to some of them at our table."

I barely heard a word she was saying.

All I could think about was the intense way Zane had stared at me when I'd walked by him earlier, and just now when we'd walked inside the dining hall.

It likely meant nothing. He was probably just wondering who the new kid on campus was, like all the other students who were trying to pretend they weren't talking about me even though they obviously were.

"So," she said. "What do you want to eat? The sushi here is surprisingly good."

"I've never had sushi before, and I'm definitely not going to try it right now," I said. "Especially since chopsticks and I don't get along." I scanned the selections again, unable to see prices anywhere. "How much does everything cost?"

"All food is included," she said, like it should have been obvious.

"Oh," I said, taken aback even after what Nicole had told me earlier about the credit cards. I'd never eaten *anywhere* without thinking about the price while deciding what to get. "How about a sandwich?"

"Sure," she said. "Sounds good."

We walked over to the sandwich line, where our sandwiches were made in front of us. It reminded me of a typical deli, but nicer.

Once we both had our food, I followed Alyssa to a table in the center of the dining hall. It was a mix of guys and girls who were dressed like they were about to attend a party instead of class. Fashionable clothing, and full-out jewelry and makeup for the girls. Alyssa blended in with them seamlessly.

Other than the coat I'd borrowed from her, I definitely didn't.

There were two empty chairs, as if they'd been saving them for us. Alyssa sat down, I did the same, and she introduced me to the six of them.

I caught the names Doreen and Parker, but the other four had already slipped my mind.

"So, you're finally stuck with a suitemate," Doreen said to Alyssa with a knowing smirk.

I froze since, judging by how friendly Alyssa had been so far, I hadn't expected her to feel that way.

"I'm not *stuck* with you," Alyssa quickly said to me, her cheeks a bright shade of pink. "I mean, I've always liked having my own bathroom. But it's totally cool. I'll figure out how to condense my stuff."

She glared at Doreen, as if saying, *What the hell did you say that for?*

Doreen seemed unfazed.

"Don't worry about it," I said to Alyssa. "I don't have much stuff. There'll be plenty of extra space on my side of the sink."

"You don't have to do that," she said. "We'll figure it out. There's actually a really cute bathroom organizer I've had my eye on for a while. I can hang it on the wall or something. It'll be fine."

"It's really not a problem," I said, and then I couldn't help myself—I looked over my shoulder at Zane and his crew of supernatural movie stars.

He was staring at me again, although he averted his eyes quickly.

My heart leaped at the energy that buzzed inside me during that split-second when our eyes locked.

Did he feel it, too? Was that why he was staring?

Probably not, given that nearly half of the students in the dining hall were staring at me.

I needed to get it together. I'd never been boy-crazy. And now—while I was trying to adapt to a school far different than anything I'd thought could possibly exist —was not the time to start.

I forced myself to refocus on Alyssa and her friends at our table.

"So," said the guy who was sitting next to Doreen. "Are you one of us?" He leaned forward, his light brown eyes studying me as he waited for a response. In his light purple polo shirt, he was as preppy as the guys at Hollins.

"You mean a descendant of Dionysus?" I asked, given that the others at the table all wore a pop of purple, too.

"Yep," he said. "Purple looks good on you."

I broke my gaze from his, not liking the way he was looking at me—like he was ready to pounce at any moment.

Maybe it was better when guys were afraid to talk to me.

"I don't know," I said quickly. "I don't even know if my element is air."

Alyssa's forehead scrunched in confusion. "What do you mean?"

Crap. I shouldn't have said that in front of everyone.

Parker had just caught me so unaware that it slipped out.

"What *do* you mean?" Doreen looked hungrier for my response than for her salad. "You took the test just like the rest of us. You tested as air. That's why you're in our dorm. Right?"

I didn't want to lie. I *hated* lying. And I was terrible at it.

I also didn't want to start off on the wrong foot with Alyssa and her friends. At least not with Alyssa, who looked as curious as the rest of them.

I might as well be out with it.

"When Nicole and Blake found me, it was because I made a bunch of crystals fly with my magic. So it's pretty clear my element is air," I repeated exactly what Kate had said. "But when I took the test, nothing happened."

"What do you mean, 'nothing happened'?" the girl whose name I couldn't remember asked.

"I couldn't move the paper. I couldn't do anything with the other elements, either."

No one said anything for a few seconds.

"Huh," Parker finally said. "Strange."

"But she's definitely not a descendent of Dionysus," Alyssa said in a clear attempt to change the subject. "I offered her a 'welcome to Elementals Academy' mimosa, and she refused."

"For sure," Parker agreed, still focused on me. "Have you had a lot of boyfriends? Or hookups?"

"Are you asking me out?" I balked. Because not only was I ridiculously inexperienced with these things, but Parker sort of reminded me of Trent.

Not my type.

Zane's mesmerizing eyes flashed through my mind.

Stop, I told myself, although my mind refused to listen.

"Nah." He shrugged. "Just asking a question."

"Her answer was definitely a no." Doreen chuckled, and she looked slightly relieved.

"Then you're probably not a descendant of Zeus," Parker continued. "They have trouble keeping it in their pants. Or *out* of their pants, if they're female."

He laughed at his own joke, and the other guy at the table chuckled, too.

Ben? Or Brad?

I really needed to get better at remembering names.

"So it's gotta be Hermes," Alyssa said, although from the way she looked at me, she didn't seem sure. "But you don't seem like a jokester. Not that we've known each other for long, but I'm usually pretty good at getting vibes from people, and you seem sort of serious. But I don't mean that as an insult," she said quickly, tripping over her words a bit. "It's just the vibe I'm getting."

I smiled, since one thing was for sure—even though Alyssa looked similar to Courtney, they weren't alike at all.

Thank God.

Or gods, given what I knew now.

"You're stuck in your head," Parker observed. "So

I'm guessing not a descendant of Hermes. Unless you're an athlete?"

"The most athletic thing I do is turn the pages of books."

"Hm." He sat back in his chair, perplexed.

"Are you sure you're in the right dorm?" Doreen asked. "Because I'm getting Athena energy here."

"She made those crystals fly," Alyssa reminded them. "That's definitely air magic." She turned back to me. "Were you nervous when you took the test?"

"That's an understatement," I said. "I didn't even know magic existed twenty-four hours ago, let alone that I had it."

"Then I'm guessing it was just nerves," she said. "But don't worry—I'll help you tap into your magic. It'll be fine."

It sounded more like she was reassuring herself than me.

"Thanks," I said. "I'd like that."

"Cool." She smiled and relaxed slightly.

"So, does everyone have traits related to their Greek ancestor?" I asked, since they were right—it wasn't that I didn't have a sense of humor, but no one would ever call me a "jokester." I also wasn't a huge partier, and I'd never hooked up with *anyone* before.

"For the most part, yes," Parker said. "But I guess there are always outliers."

"Outliers?" I repeated. "Is that just a polite way of saying 'freaks of nature'?"

He grinned. "Maybe you're more of a jokester than you seem."

If that was how he translated "sarcasm," then sure. Just call me the clown of the circus.

And despite what Nicole had said about me belonging at Elementals Academy, it was feeling unlikely that I'd fit in better at this school than I had at any other.

CHAPTER TWELVE

I wasn't sure what was more unreal—the magic of Elementals Academy, or the fact that all the students had basically unlimited money at their disposal. Shopping with Nicole was something else. She didn't even look at the price tags before telling the saleslady to bring something to the dressing room. I felt awkward allowing someone to bring my clothes to the dressing room for me, but Nicole insisted upon it.

Then there were the dressing rooms themselves. There were three-way mirrors with little pedestals to stand on, and perfect lighting. It was nothing like the fluorescent lighting in TJ Maxx that made you look terrible.

When we checked out, the saleslady brought us to a private little room with its own cash register. One t-shirt cost more than a month's worth of groceries, and a single pair of jeans was rent.

I was stepping from one alternate reality to the next.

But Nicole was friendly and fun, and I was grateful for her and Alyssa. She helped me bring my *multiple* shopping bags to my room, which, as promised, was now full of my stuff from home. The Elders sure knew how to "take care of things" quickly—which was further proven by the text from my mom asking how I was liking my new school. I'd quickly messaged her that all was well, and she didn't mention that I was supposed to come home after the test yesterday. It was like she'd forgotten.

Maybe she had.

When Nicole came inside with me, Alyssa gaped at her like she was a celebrity.

"Nicole Cassidy," she squealed. "Omigod. Hi! Are you coming to the around the world party tonight?"

"I'm heading to the city with Blake," she said. "But maybe we'll stop by later."

"Awesome!" Alyssa said. "You should totally come to my room first. I made my signature sangria."

"Sounds great," Nicole said in a tone that made it sound like she probably wasn't making it to the party. Then she glanced at her watch. "Hey, I've gotta run. Have fun tonight!"

Alyssa watched Nicole with wide eyes as she headed

out. Once the door was closed, she turned to me and said, "I can't believe she's coming to the party tonight."

"Why?" I asked, even though I was pretty sure Nicole wasn't going to show up.

"She doesn't usually come to parties. On the weekends, she and Blake and some of the more powerful witches go to the city and surrounding areas to take care of any potential threats, like the harpy that attacked you at your apartment."

Of course. Monsters.

"How many are out there?" I asked.

"No idea." She shrugged. "A lot of them stay in hiding, but the more humanoid ones can blend into society. DC and the surrounding areas are clear of them, thanks to Nicole and Blake. It's why it's safe for us to go out to the city."

"They did take down that harpy pretty quickly," I said.

"Of course they did. They're the best fighters around. I'm sure Nicole told you all about it while you were shopping."

"Not really," I said. "She mainly tried to catch me up on what I missed in my classes. She said she was behind when she first learned she was a witch, and she wanted to make sure I went in as armed as possible. Although I don't think anything will prepare me for the magical training classes. Those sound tough."

"I told you I'd help you," Alyssa said. "But are you telling me that Nicole said *nothing* about what she and the original Elementals did?"

"No..."

"They saved the world." She said it as casually as if she'd told me what they served in the dining hall for lunch. "She and the other Elementals got their magic at the same time as a portal to a prison realm opened. The prison realm contained the Titans, who wanted to kill the Olympian gods. But the Elementals used their magic to stop the most dangerous Titan of all—Typhon—and they closed the portal to the prison realm to stop the Titans from returning. They're legends around here."

"Wow," I said. "She definitely didn't mention any of that."

"Well, now you know," she said. "And now, it's time that *I* know what you bought at the mall. Because we need to figure out what you're wearing to the party tonight."

Alyssa was *not* excited about the clothes I'd picked out with Nicole. Probably because they were mostly black, and Alyssa was all about pops of color.

For the party, I went with my signature favorite—tight black jeans with a black tank top that showed a hint of my midriff. It was hard to go wrong with all black. And since the party was in the dorm, I didn't have to worry about figuring out how to layer my new winter gear.

I *did* let Alyssa do my makeup, since she was so excited about it. I didn't normally wear a lot of makeup, but I had to admit that the black winged eyeliner looked good with the outfit.

"This is a great opportunity to meet people from the other dorms," she said after sizing me up and determining that I was officially ready.

"Why don't I just stay in the room with you?" I asked. "You can introduce me to everyone as they come around."

I'd never heard of an "around the world" party, but Alyssa had been quick to fill me in this morning. This afternoon, each descendant of Dionysus had made a different drink—one that was their specialty. Tonight, everyone else—including students from other dorms— would go from room to room, socializing while trying each drink.

"I'll meet as many people in your room as I would by going to the other rooms," I added.

"That ruins the fun of it." She pouted. "I want you to have a good time. And it's *fun* to try all the drinks! Just give it a chance. If you're miserable, you can come back to my room. Or back to your room, but then you'll *totally* miss out on the fun."

I didn't know about that, since I'd definitely have fun finishing the book I was currently reading.

On the other hand, I didn't want to continue being an outcast here. Which meant not holing myself up in my room all night.

"I'll start in your room," I decided. "If one of your friends wants to take me around to the others, then I won't say no."

"Yay!" Alyssa jumped and clapped her hands together. "I can totally arrange that. Now… how about a pre-game drink?"

"I'm about to drink around the world," I said, even though for me, it would probably be "take a few sips at each room" around the world. "I don't think I need anything before the party starts."

"Well, I need someone to taste my sangria." She reached for my hand and pulled me into her room, where I did as she'd asked. But only a sip.

Like she'd claimed, it was excellent.

Hopefully the party would be excellent, too.

CHAPTER THIRTEEN

Alyssa was quick to text a friend of hers to ask her to take me "around the world" with her—a fun, lighthearted girl named Jamie with dark skin, bright brown eyes, and braided hair. She was beautiful and radiant, and I would have thought she was a descendant of Aphrodite if I didn't already know she lived in our dorm.

"This is Summer," Alyssa introduced me to Jamie. "She's never been to an around the world party before, and she's *super* shy."

"I'm not 'super shy,'" I said quickly. "I'm just not used to people being so nice."

"Said like a girl who grew up not knowing she's a witch," Jamie said.

"It's that obvious?"

"Everyone at school knows. But I was the same. So don't worry—I've got your back."

"Thanks," I said.

"Anytime." Jamie paused to size me up. "I'm happy to finally meet the girl who's captured every guy in the academy's heart."

"What are you talking about?"

"The guys won't stop talking about you," she said. "Especially the descendants of Zeus. The guys have a bet —" She cut herself off, but from the way her eyes twinkled, I had a feeling she'd planned to leave me hanging.

"They're out of luck." I rolled my eyes. "I'm not into man-whores."

"Hey." Jamie feigned like she was offended. "Descendants of Zeus aren't *all* that bad."

My heart stopped. "You're one of them?"

"Yep."

"Sorry," I said quickly. "I didn't realize."

"Don't worry about it," she brushed it off. "I don't take much personally. But the girls are pretty jealous. Especially the descendants of Zeus."

"But not you?" I asked.

"I'm not the jealous type. Anyway, I have a boyfriend," she said. "He's at the library working on a paper. It's not due until Monday, but he's a descendant of Athena, so he's super obsessed with school." She rolled her eyes, as if she was expecting me to agree with how lame it was.

"I know a thing or two about spending time at the library on weekend nights," I said instead.

Jamie narrowed her eyes in suspicion. "Are you *sure* you don't belong in the earth dorm?"

"I have no idea where I belong." I shrugged.

"I do," Alyssa said. "You belong here, at this party tonight." She shot me a smile, then walked to her door and opened it. "My room's open!" she shouted down the hall. "Who wants some sangria?!"

In what felt like an instant, five people flooded into her room.

She immediately began ladling sangria from the punch bowl into Solo cups and handing them out.

"Want some?" she asked, handing a cup to me.

"I already had some earlier," I reminded her. "And I won't be able to taste the other drinks if I get drunk in my first room."

"Good point." She nodded, apparently satisfied with my reasoning.

"Give me one," Jamie said, and then she gulped down half of it and took my hand. "Come on—I've heard the drink in Parker's room is to *die* for. Let's grab some before it's gone."

I could barely say goodbye to Alyssa before we were out the door.

I could barely taste whatever drink Jamie had thrown into my hand in Parker's room.

Because right after taking my first sip, *he* stepped inside.

Zane.

His ice-blue eyes locked with mine, sending shivers down my spine. But just like at lunch yesterday, he quickly looked away.

Like me, he also wore all black. And he was with the Barbie girl—Vera.

"Wow," Jamie whispered in my ear, her breath already rife with vodka. "I didn't expect *him* to be here."

"Who?" I turned to her, making sure my back was facing Zane.

"Zane Caldwell," she said, and my heart leaped when she spoke his name. "He never comes to parties. I'm pretty sure he stays away from the air dorm because all the female descendants of Zeus have their eyes on him. Some male ones, too."

Jealousy surged through me at the thought of how many descendants of Zeus would be all over him tonight —and at how Vera was glaring at anyone who looked at him, like a territorial cat.

Not that it was any of my business who he talked to, since we'd never said a word to each other.

"I don't like this drink," I said suddenly to Jamie. "Let's check out the next room?"

She tilted her head, confused. "Sure," she said, and then she led us out into the hallway.

We only walked a few steps before she stopped and turned toward me. She was still holding the red Solo cup full of whatever Parker was serving in his room.

"What?" I asked.

"You got all weird when Zane walked in," she said bluntly. "Did something happen between you two?"

"I've never talked to him in my life," I said.

"But you think he's hot. I could tell by the way you looked at him."

My cheeks heated, but I took a deep breath, determined to play it cool. "Of course I think he's hot," I said. "I'm sure *everyone* thinks he's hot."

"True," she agreed. "So why'd you want to leave?"

"I told you—I didn't like that drink," I said, since admitting that I didn't like watching him talk to another girl was too lame. "Let's keep going?"

"Sounds good," she said, although from the way she said it, I could tell she didn't believe me.

———

Jamie continued leading me from room to room.

With each room we entered, it was only a few

minutes before Zane appeared as well, with Vera by his side.

Was he following us?

Probably not. People were all moving in the same direction "around the world." He was just following the same pattern as everyone else.

Still, I had the constant feeling that someone was watching me. But whenever I turned around to see if it was Zane, his attention was on Vera, or on whatever he was drinking.

He was pounding down twice as many drinks as everyone else, but he wasn't getting sloppy. Trent and the other frat guys at Hollins probably would have found it beyond impressive.

Speaking of sloppy, Jamie had gotten to that point two drinks ago. She was now sitting on the lap of a guy with muscles clearly built from hours in the gym, and her cleavage was shoved in his face.

If I were her boyfriend, I would *not* be happy with her right now.

I stood awkwardly in the corner next to them, scrolling through social media on my phone, trying to look busy.

The next thing I knew, someone was standing in front of me. A tall, tan guy with muscles bigger than the guy Jamie was talking to. With his long hair and facial hair, he was going for the Jason Momoa look, but the predatory way he was staring at me was more scary than attractive.

He placed his hand on the wall next to my shoulder, towering over me in a complete invasion of my personal space.

"New girl," he said, his breath reeking of alcohol. "Autumn, right?" His fiery gaze dropped down to study my cleavage, and he licked his lips, like he was looking at his next meal.

"Wrong season." I glared up at him, figuring he'd get the point and back off.

All he did was move closer. "I'm Drake. Demigod son of Ares," he said.

"And I was just about to leave," I said, since I'd had enough of this party, and every instinct of mine was telling me to get away from this guy.

I tried to shimmy around him, but he blocked my way.

"Excuse me," I said, clearing my throat in annoyance.

"You still have half your drink left," he said.

"I'm done."

"But I'm not done with you." He stepped closer to me and rubbed himself up against me.

Disgust surged through me, and something to the side crashed to the ground. A jewelry box. It had opened like a tipped treasure chest, with necklaces and bracelets spilling out of it.

The next thing I knew, something squishy and slimy traveled from my jawline up to my ear.

Drake was *licking* me.

"Get *off*." I pushed at his chest, but it was like he was built of steel. He didn't move.

"Relax," he said, his breath hot in my ear. "Have a little fun."

"Get. Off. Me." With nothing else left at my disposal, I emptied the contents of my punch onto his white shirt.

"Bitch." He sneered.

I was getting ready to try to shove him out of my way again when a hand wrapped around one of his wrists and flung him into the opposite wall, so high that his head nearly hit the ceiling.

He slammed into the concrete blocks with a loud crash, then fell to the bed below him. The wall near the ceiling—where his back had hit—was cracked. He groaned and moved a bit, so at least he wasn't dead.

Zane stood next to me, rage brewing in his ice-cold eyes as he glared at Drake.

Everyone else in the room was silent, and they stared at Zane, then Drake, then back again.

Zane ignored them and reached for my hand. His skin was surprisingly cool. Not cold, but definitely not as warm as it should have been.

My heart leaped, and I froze under his gaze. It was like he'd cast a spell on me.

"Come on," he said, his voice smooth and controlled.

"Zane," Vera said as he pushed past her. "What are you—"

"I've got it under control," he growled, then he looked back to me and continued, "Let's get you out of here."

CHAPTER FOURTEEN

Zane pushed past two students in the hall and hurried us toward the front door.

The second we reached the foyer, I pulled my hand out of his and faced him.

He was eerily calm—the type of calm someone got when they were doing everything possible to stop themselves from exploding with anger. His breaths were slow and steady, and his ice-blue eyes stared intensely down at me.

"Why did you do that?" I asked, somehow composing myself enough to speak.

"You wanted him off of you," he said. "So I got him off of you."

"You broke the wall."

"Drake's an asshole," he said. "And no one else has

the courage to stand up to the demigod son of Ares. So I took care of him for you."

"Why?" I asked again. "You don't even know me."

"You're Summer Donovan," he said, his hypnotizing gaze locked on mine. "You came here yesterday from Winter Park, Florida. Everyone's curious about you because you got your magic after the semester started, and you wish they'd all stop staring and whispering, because you don't like being the center of attention. You're more reserved than any other student here gifted with magic over air, and you don't fit in with them at all. Your left hand is your dominant hand, and you play with the tips of your fingers on your right hand when you're nervous. And apparently, you have a hard time saying thank you."

I stilled, surprised by how much he'd noticed about me, then dropped my hands to my sides. Because I'd definitely been playing with the fingers of my right hand, and I was most definitely nervous around him. The excited type of nervous, but it was embarrassing that he'd noticed.

"Thank you," I finally said, and I wiped my cheek where Drake had licked me.

My skin there felt contaminated. I was going to have to scrub it raw tonight.

"You're welcome." Zane gave me the semblance of a smile and reached for my hand again. "Let's go."

"My room's up there." I glanced at the spiral staircase, although I dreaded going back to the suite I shared with Alyssa. Because while I had a room to myself, it was still connected by the bathroom linking her room to mine. Everyone would hear when I jumped into the shower, and I didn't want them checking on me and trying to convince me to re-join the party.

Even more so, I didn't want *Drake* to come looking for me.

"You're coming back with me," he said simply.

My eyes widened in surprise. "You mean to the water dorm?"

"That's where my room is," he confirmed, and then he reached to open the door to leave the dorm.

I stepped back, pulling my hand out of his.

The moment I did, I regretted it. Because I kind of liked holding his hand. No—I *really* liked it. His touch might not have been warm, but it was strangely comforting.

"We've literally only said a few sentences to each other." I somehow got my wits together, even though my heart fluttered more at the thought of going *anywhere* with Zane. "If you think I'm going to hook up with you because you rescued me from Drake, then you thought wrong."

"I never assumed anything," he said coolly. "Like you said, we don't know each other. But I *do* know that your room is connected to Alyssa's through your shared bathroom, which has locks on the inside but not the outside. And I know Drake's pissed off, because he's not used to being rejected. I wouldn't put it past him to go into Alyssa's room—which is open to party guests—and try to go through the shared bathroom to find you in your room."

I shuddered at the thought of my space being invaded like that.

Especially because I'd already thought the same thing about my room being connected to Alyssa's, which meant I wasn't being totally paranoid about it.

He watched me, waiting.

I started playing with the tips of my fingers again, then realized and stopped.

"What about Vera?" I asked. "She didn't seem happy that you were leaving with me."

"Vera's an old family friend," he said. "Besides, this isn't about her. It's about you."

"You *really* want me to come back with you, don't you?" I joked to try to diffuse the tension, which was so intense that it felt like a living thing between us.

"I just want you to be safe," he said, more serious than ever.

I wanted to say that I was safe in the academy. But after the incident with Drake, I wasn't so sure. Especially given how many drunk people were stumbling around the dorm tonight.

"Why?" I asked.

"Because you don't know how to control your magic yet."

"How do you know that?"

"Everyone knows it after you told Alyssa's friends in the cafeteria yesterday," he said. "Important advice—don't tell Doreen anything you don't want the entire school to know."

I sighed, since I'd pretty much known that after it had slipped out.

"I do have magic," I said. "I think I made that jewelry box tip over."

"I said you don't know how to *control* your magic—not that you don't have it," he said. "What good would a fallen jewelry box have done against Drake?"

"Nothing," I admitted. "But it still doesn't explain why you've taken it upon yourself to help me."

"I took it upon myself when I yanked that asshole off you and threw him into a wall." Fury swirled in his eyes, as if thinking about it made him angry all over again. "And I like to finish things I start."

My breathing shallowed. Because for some unknown reason, Zane was being protective over me. And for another unknown reason, I *liked* it.

All my instincts told me to trust him.

"You're not going to let this go, are you?" I asked.

"Is that a yes?" he challenged, electricity humming between us.

"Maybe." I looked him up and down, since there was one more thing that wasn't adding up. "But how come you aren't drunk?"

"What do you mean?"

"I mean that I noticed things about you tonight, too. Including that you had almost twice as much to drink as most of the people here. But you seem totally sober."

My head buzzed—a reminder that while I'd tried to pace myself, I'd drank more at the party than I was used to. Not so much that I wasn't in control of myself, but still enough to be tipsy. Lara's voice calling me a light-weight sounded in my mind.

"I have a high alcohol tolerance," he said simply.

"Does it have to do with being a water elemental?"

"It's genetics." He shrugged. "But don't worry—I'll be sleeping on the couch. The bed is yours."

I bit my lower lip as I thought about it. The only other friend I had here was Nicole, but she and Blake were doing their superhero thing in the city. And while Kate had been warm and welcoming, she was the head-mistress of the school—not a friend. Plus, she was probably asleep.

"Fine," I said. "I'll stay with you."

The moment the words were out of my mouth, I realized how crazy they were. Because I had no reason to think Zane was any better than Drake. What if he tried to do what Drake had done in the open behind closed doors?

But looking up into his caring, hopeful eyes, I knew that wasn't the case. For some unknown reason, he was truly protecting me. He'd proven that by what he'd done to Drake.

"Are you sure?" he asked, which solidified my instinct.

"Yes," I said. "But will you come with me while I grab a jacket? I don't want to freeze out there."

"Of course," he said. "Let's get it, then get out of here."

CHAPTER FIFTEEN

I changed into sweatpants and a sweatshirt when I got my jacket, since I didn't want to sleep in my jeans. Not the sexiest thing ever, but it was comfortable.

Besides, it didn't matter if I dressed sexy or not. Because I wasn't going to hook up with Zane on the night we'd met, no matter how alluring he might be.

"How are you not freezing?" I asked Zane as we made our way to the water dorm, since he was only wearing a t-shirt and it felt cold enough to snow.

Not that I knew what it felt like to be cold enough to snow. But given that I could see my breath when I spoke, I figured it was like this.

"I'm a water elemental," he said simply. "And my specialty is ice."

He stopped walking, then held his hands up so his palms were facing each other, with a little less than a foot between them. The space between them shimmered, flashed pale blue, and then he was holding a perfectly smooth, clear sphere about the size of a tennis ball between them. It rotated around, and droplets swirled out of it like a kaleidoscope, slithering between his fingers and freezing mid-air.

His eyes looked icier under the glow of the crescent moon.

"Wow." I reached forward to touch it, but stopped myself. Touching his creation felt personal, and I didn't feel right doing it without his permission.

"You can touch." His gaze was locked with mine, and there was a dangerous edge to his tone—like he was breaking a rule.

"Are you sure?" I asked.

"I'm sure."

I continued to reach forward, then brushed the pads of my fingers against his creation.

The ball in the center was solid ice, and it was just as smooth as it looked.

He watched me as I slid my fingers over it, and the moment felt strangely intimate. I somehow felt cold and on fire all at the same time.

And I was completely hypnotized by his gaze. It felt like an invisible force was drawing us toward one another—a force stronger than magic. He leaned forward as well, so close that the puffs of our breath in the cold air were nearly touching.

I'd told him that nothing would happen between us if we went back to his room. But if he kissed me right now, I didn't think I'd be able to resist.

Turned out I didn't have to worry about it, because he looked away, stepped back, and released his hold on his magic. It turned to water and splashed to the ground.

I blinked a few times to orient myself.

"Come on," he said, breaking the moment between us. "I might be immune to the cold, but I don't want you to freeze to death."

He hurried as he led the way to the water dorm, both of us silent. I had no idea what to say to him after that almost-kiss, and every time I glanced his way, he was looking forward, as if I wasn't even there.

The water dorm was about the same size as the air dorm, except the word NEPO was carved above the door. I assumed it was the Greek word for water.

He held his watch up to the scanner, the door clicked as it unlocked, and he opened it for me.

I stepped into a foyer with dark wood floors, deep blue walls, and a chandelier that looked like it was made of icicles. It was colder than the air dorm, and I was glad I'd put on a sweatshirt.

"I'm this way," he said, and he led the way down the hall on the first floor, to a room on the left.

Luckily, we didn't run into anyone on our way there. It was that time of night when people were either out partying or in their rooms sleeping. Which was a good thing, since they would have definitely thought that my going back to Zane's room was something it wasn't.

Although after that near-kiss outside, I had no idea *what* it was.

He opened his door, which led into a room the same size as mine, with the same basic furniture. Besides a few photos of snowy mountains and glaciers hanging on the wall, he hadn't gone out of his way to decorate.

He took my jacket and hung it on the coat stand next to the door.

I looked at one of the photos of a glacier. "Those are pretty," I said.

"Thanks," he said. "They were gifts."

"From who?"

He paused, as if the question had tripped him up. "From my father."

"Cool." I started playing with my fingers again, then caught myself and stopped. "Where are you from?"

"Up north," he said. "Vermont."

Somehow, we were standing closer to each other than we'd been a minute ago.

Had I been the one who'd moved forward, or had he?

I glanced down, my cheeks heating. "Did you know

you were a witch before coming here?" I asked, trying to diffuse the tension. "Or were you like me?"

A *lost witch*, the words Kate had said replayed in my mind.

Except I hadn't technically gotten lost.

I'd been abandoned.

It was something I'd grown to accept as I'd gotten older. But now that I knew my parents were witches, it was like the wound had re-opened. Because they'd given me up *knowing* they wouldn't be there to teach me about this huge part of who I was.

They knew I'd need them, but they'd left me there anyway.

Knowing that hurt me deep in my soul.

"I've always known I had magic," Zane said. "Although I haven't been claimed by my godly ancestor yet."

I nodded, remembering Alyssa had mentioned that at lunch yesterday.

"But they assume you're a descendant of Aphrodite," I said. "Because of how—"

I cut myself off before I could say, *how attractive you are.*

He raised an eyebrow in amusement. "Because of how what?"

"Nothing," I said quickly, searching for a way to change the subject. "Do you think someone in the academy will be able to track down my parents? Like how they found me after I used magic?"

"They're only able to track down elemental witches." He frowned, looking sad for me. "So I don't think so."

I had a feeling that would be the answer, since Kate had basically told me the same thing when I'd gotten to the school.

My gaze wandered to his bookshelf, since my eyes always eventually found their way to bookshelves. He had lots of books—more than just the ones supplied by the academy. Greek myths, Roman myths, Norse myths, Egyptian myths, and some general mythology textbooks.

"We learn about mythology that isn't Greek?" I asked, surprised.

"No," he said. "But I have broad interests. I also think this game of twenty questions should end until after you get some rest. You've had a long night."

"I'm not tired," I said, even though the alcohol I'd consumed was definitely catching up to me. I felt a yawn creeping up, and failed to suppress it.

"Convincing." He smirked. "Tell you what—you can ask me whatever you want tomorrow. But right now, I have a challenge for you."

"What type of challenge?" I studied him, ready for anything.

"Get under the covers and close your eyes for ten

minutes," he said. "If you're still awake after that, we can chat more."

I narrowed my eyes at him. "I'm not ten years old."

His gaze traveled up and down my body. "I've noticed," he said, and I felt my cheeks flush. "You also drank a lot tonight, so you have that tipsy look in your eyes."

"I do not," I said, even though I probably did.

"You're free to take a look." He motioned to the full-length mirror that was identical to mine.

I stepped up to the mirror and looked at my reflection, embarrassed to see that not only did I have that "tipsy look in my eyes," but also that my mascara had flaked below them. I rubbed at it to fix it, but it only resulted in little smears.

Suddenly, prickles traveled over my arms and down my spine. And not the exciting ones I felt whenever Zane looked at me.

These felt like an inexplicable invasion of privacy.

I quickly stepped away from the mirror and turned back around to face Zane.

"So, what do you say?" he asked, looking proud of himself. "Are you up for the challenge?"

Centering myself, I shook off that weird feeling I'd had while looking into the mirror. Which was easy to do, since being around Zane made me feel strangely safe.

He studied me, waiting for my answer.

"Fine," I huffed, removed my sheepskin boots, and got into the bed.

His bed.

My heart raced from thinking about it.

It picked up the pace even more when I realized he was watching me like I was the most precious thing in the world. Like he truly cared about me, even though we'd just met.

Maybe I should tell him he didn't have to sleep on the couch? I imagined it would be nice to share a bed with him. Comfortable. Safe.

Before I could decide, he walked over to the light switch and turned it off. The only light that remained on was the soft one from the lamp next to the couch.

"Goodnight, Summer," he murmured, and he smirked slightly, like he'd already won.

"Don't underestimate me," I replied. "I'm going to pass your challenge."

"All right." He tapped on his watch a few times. "The timer starts now."

"Talk to you in ten minutes," I said, and then I laid down, rested my head on the pillow, and closed my eyes.

Stay up, I told myself.

But sleep took me nearly instantly.

CHAPTER SIXTEEN

I woke up and glanced at my watch.

It was 6:00 AM.

And I was currently in Zane's bed, while he was sound asleep on the couch. He looked so at peace, and even though I wanted to continue our conversation from last night, I didn't want to wake him.

So I got out of bed as quietly as I could, grabbed my boots and jacket, and tiptoed to the door.

I held my breath as I unlocked the deadbolt, praying it wouldn't make any noise. It didn't. Neither did the hinges when I opened the door and shut it behind me.

I stood still, prepared for Zane to open the door to come after me. But nothing happened.

Confident that I hadn't woken him, I put on my boots and jacket, pulled the hood over my head, and hurried out of the dorm. There were barely any students walking around outside, since it was 6:00 AM on a Saturday morning.

Finally, I got back to the air dorm.

It was a mess. The common room had red Solo cups strewn about, as did the halls. The entire place reeked of alcohol.

Hopefully this party was a special one for the start of the semester, and not a regular occurrence. God help me if it was. Because despite my element being air, I most definitely didn't fit in with the others in this dorm.

The first thing I did when I got back to my room was take a shower, as if the hot water could wash off the memory of the places Drake had touched me. Afterward, I dried off, tied the towel around myself like a toga, and examined Alyssa's beauty products crammed into her side of the sink. It took about a minute to find exfoliator.

I used it on the cheek that Drake had licked until I'd scrubbed my skin raw.

As I examined it in the mirror, the same prickly feeling passed over me that I'd felt last night. But before I could think about it further, there was a knock on the door that led to Alyssa's room.

"Summer?" she asked. "Are you okay?"

I used the washcloth to dry my face, then unlocked the door and opened it.

Alyssa looked awful. Her eyeliner was smudged, and her blond hair had some streaks of red in it that were strikingly similar to the color of the sangria she'd served last night. Her massive t-shirt hung over her frame so loosely that she looked like a child.

"Why are you up this early?" I asked, although from the looks of her, a better question would have been *how* she was up this early.

"I heard you come in," she said, and her eyes sparkled despite how tired she looked. "So? How'd it go with Zane?"

"Oh my God," I said. "Does everyone know?"

"He threw Drake into a wall, dragged you out of the room, and then the two of you left the dorm together. So, yeah. Everyone knows. Anyway—how'd it go?"

"Nothing happened." I shrugged.

"What do you mean *nothing happened?*"

"He was just worried about me after the whole Drake incident," I said. "He didn't want Drake to try barging into my room or something, so he offered to let me crash with him for the night. We chatted for a bit, then I slept on the bed, and he slept on the couch. I woke up before he did, and now I'm back here."

"That's it?"

"Yeah. That's it."

"Hm." She looked genuinely perplexed. "Do you think he's gay?"

The memory of the way he'd looked at me when he'd shown me his ice magic flashed through my mind—when I'd sworn he was going to kiss me. "Nope," I said. "Definitely not gay."

"Then are *you?*" she asked. "Because any girl on campus would love to go back to Zane Caldwell's room. And no way did he bring you back there just to sleep."

"No." I huffed and rolled my eyes at how quickly she'd jumped to conclusions.

"Not like it would be a problem if you were," she quickly followed up. "Although I'm pretty sure it would disappoint the entire straight male population at this school. But if something *did* happen between you and Zane, I get it if you don't want to say anything. I totally respect your privacy. But if you do want to talk, I'm always here to listen."

She somehow managed to get that out without taking a single breath.

"Thanks," I said. "I appreciate that."

"Anyway, the Drake thing was crazy," she continued. "Zane threw him so hard that he cracked the wall. The *cement* wall."

"I guess that's what happens when witches get into fights?" I shrugged.

"No," she said. "We're strong, but not *that* strong. And Drake's a demigod, which makes him one of the strongest witches at the school. The fact that Zane could do that is insane. People were checking out the crack in the wall all night to make sure it was real."

"Zane hasn't been claimed by his godly ancestor yet," I reminded her. "Maybe he's a demigod, too."

"Maybe," she said. "But tell me—did he at least give you his number?"

"He didn't." I frowned, disappointed. "We didn't really have time for that."

"Because you were busy doing *other* things?" She waggled her eyebrows.

I sighed in frustration. "The entire school's gonna think we hooked up, aren't they?"

"Yep. Absolutely. But that's not a bad thing. People hook up here all the time. I'm sure they'll forget about it in a week."

She didn't sound very convincing.

"Anyways, I'm tired," she said with a big yawn. "Let's order pizza later? I'm gonna need some greasy food to soak up this hangover."

"Dominos or Papa Johns?" I asked.

"Dominos, all the way."

"I knew I liked you," I said.

"You bet." She smiled. "And I'm sure you need some rest, too."

"I told you—we just slept." I rolled my eyes again.

"Sure you did." She stuck her tongue out and closed the door, giving me a wink before it clicked shut.

If I'd had any chance of blending in, I'd definitely lost it last night.

But as I thought back to the time I'd spent with Zane, I realized I didn't regret a single thing.

CHAPTER SEVENTEEN

My schedule appeared on the Elementals Academy app last night, while Alyssa and I were polishing off our pizza. I was in the same classes as her, which were basic gen-ed classes for freshmen. Quantitative reasoning, art history, and English 101. Nothing that sounded too difficult, which I was grateful for, given how much I needed to learn about being a witch.

In the afternoons, we had History of Magic on Tuesdays and Thursdays, and elemental training on Mondays, Wednesdays, and Fridays. History of Magic was only for freshmen, and elemental training was only for air elementals.

Given that Zane was a junior and a water elemental, the chance of us having any gen-ed classes together was slim-to-none. Which was probably a good thing, because

I doubted I'd be able to focus on what we were learning if he was in the room.

Alyssa sat with me in each class, and beside the fact that a bunch of students looked at me and whispered when we arrived—I definitely heard Drake and Zane's names mentioned—the classes were pretty normal. Quantitative reasoning (math) hurt my brain a bit, and I resented having it first thing in the morning. Art history was fascinating, and English 101 was easy.

But I could barely focus during English. The notes document on my laptop was basically blank. All I could think about was what would happen when I saw Zane at lunch.

Would he ask me to join his table? Would he come sit at mine? Would he be waiting outside the dining hall so we could go through the food line together, and ask to sit alone with me?

A message popped up on my screen. From Alyssa.

You okay?

Yeah, I replied. *Why?*

You look spaced out.

Great. If Alyssa could tell, my professor probably could, too. Hopefully she'd think I was just over-whelmed by starting at the academy.

But Alyssa was my friend, and I wanted to be honest with her.

I keep thinking about Zane. I'm kinda anxious about what's gonna happen when I see him at lunch.

It'll go great! she replied quickly.

My fingers hovered over the keys, and she glanced over at me, waiting for a response.

I didn't realize that witches could be psychics too, I finally replied.

We're not. But you're hot AF. I bet he's counting down the seconds until he sees you again.

Thanks, I replied and then I brought my notes app back up and did my best to focus for the rest of the class.

***

Jamie joined me and Alyssa on our walk to the dining hall.

"I'm so sorry for what happened at the party," she said. "I had a lot to drink, and I thought you were into Drake. If I knew you weren't, I totally would have helped you escape."

"She didn't need your help," Alyssa jumped in. "She had Zane's."

I inwardly cringed at how Alyssa brought it up. She didn't mean any harm—and it wasn't like she was telling Jamie anything that the entire school didn't already know—but I didn't feel like rehashing what I'd told Alyssa yesterday.

People were going to think what they wanted to think, and I didn't want to spin the gossip wheel any faster than it already was going.

"Don't worry about it," I told Jamie. "We're cool."

"Cool." Relief flashed across her face. "But Drake's *the* strongest student at this school. What Zane did to him was crazy."

"Our working theory is that Zane's a demigod," Alyssa said.

"That would make sense," Jamie said, and then she looked to me. "Did you know him before coming here?"

"He's from Vermont, and I'd never left Florida before a few days ago," I said. "So, no. We just met."

"I've never seen Zane go out of his way to help anyone," she continued. "Or to talk to anyone. Except for Vera."

"They're old family friends," I said quickly.

"Interesting." She eyed me, and I got that pit in the bottom of my stomach about what she was going to ask next.

The same thing most people were wondering—what had happened when we'd gotten back to his room.

"Zane and I are just friends," I said before she could ask. "He helped me get away from Drake, and I appreciated it. That's all."

"Oookay," Jamie said, and then Alyssa switched the topic to some other piece of gossip that had happened during the party, and I spent the rest of the walk to the dining hall wondering what was going to happen when I saw Zane at lunch.

CHAPTER EIGHTEEN

Zane sat at the back table where he'd been on Friday, with the group of descendants of Aphrodite.

I froze the moment I saw him.

Should I go over there and say hi? Wait for him to wave me over?

Do something other than standing there paralyzed?

I groaned inwardly at how much I was over-analyzing all of it. Someone with more experience with this sort of thing would know what to do. Then there was me—social pariah for my entire life. Totally clueless in all things that had to do with guys.

Finally, his eyes met mine.

His expression glazed over into total ambivalence, and he turned away to say something to Vera.

My breath caught in my chest. I waited for him to look back at me, but he was acting like I wasn't there.

"Wow," Jamie said. "That was cold."

I couldn't form words for a few seconds.

"I don't get it," I finally said.

"Guys are assholes," Alyssa said. "Come on. Let's get our food."

I felt like I was walking in slow motion, replaying everything that had happened Saturday night in my mind. "I left before he woke up," I said. "Maybe he thought I was blowing him off?"

"Did you leave a note?" Alyssa asked.

"No. I didn't want to wake him up."

"Did you text him?" Jamie asked.

"I don't have his number."

"Hm." She pressed her lips together, then shrugged. "You should talk to him."

"Now?"

"No!" Alyssa looked at Jamie like she was crazy, then turned back to me. "Is that the sort of conversation you want to have in front of everyone at his table?"

"Not really." I felt like an idiot for not having thought of that—especially since Vera was sitting next to him. "I guess I'll try to catch him when he leaves."

My stomach flipped at the thought. Because he hadn't looked hurt when he'd met my eyes—he'd looked like he didn't even know me.

Like I was a ghost.

My appetite was totally gone. There was no way I'd be able to sit there for the entirety of lunch and eat, knowing he was in the dining hall ignoring me.

"Screw that," I said. "I'm talking to him now."

Jamie smirked. "That's the spirit!"

I took a deep breath.

I didn't imagine the connection between us on Saturday night, I reminded myself. *He felt it, too. I know he did.*

So I straightened my shoulders, held my head up high, and marched toward Zane's table.

They all quieted as I approached.

Vera rolled her eyes.

Zane met my gaze with indifference. His eyes that had been so inviting Saturday night were now as icy as their color. It was like he was a different person, and my heart dropped with the feeling that this was *not* going to go well.

But I was already there, and I wasn't going to back down now.

"Can we talk?" I asked him.

"Sure." He leaned calmly back in his seat. "Talk."

"Alone."

He didn't say anything for a few seconds.

He's going to say no.

My heart pounded so hard that it felt like it was

going to burst out of my chest, and the voices of everyone in the dining hall sounded muffled.

What would I do if he said no?

Beg him to talk to me alone? Say what I'd come over here to say in front of everyone at his table?

The anxiety continued to grow inside me, and I held his gaze, silently begging him to not embarrass me in front of everyone there.

He pushed his chair back so forcibly that the metal legs screeched across the floor. "Fine," he said, standing up. "Where do you want to talk?"

"Um…" I glanced around, since I hadn't thought that far ahead yet. "Outside?"

His eyes danced in amusement, and he motioned to the door that led to the back patio. "Lead the way."

I spun around and headed toward the door, praying he'd do as he said and follow me. I looked over my shoulder after getting there, relieved to see him slightly behind.

He reached across me to open the door, and his hand brushed my arm in the process.

Heat rushed through my body, and he took a sharp breath inward. But when I looked back up at him, his eyes were as icy and uncaring as ever.

He pushed the door open, and the cold air rushed toward me, freezing my cheeks that had just been starting to warm back up.

That was why no one was eating outside.

In my moment of panic, I'd replied to his question about where we should go to chat as automatically as I would have in Florida, where the outside didn't present a constant risk of contracting hypothermia.

"After you," he said, sounding frustratingly amused.

I wrapped my arms around myself, grateful for my warm fleece, and walked to a spot that wasn't visible through the window.

Once there, I spun around to face him.

He waited, his expression still ambivalent.

Maybe this was how Zane reacted when someone hurt him? Put up a wall so no one could tell?

I decided to go with that.

"I'm sorry I left yesterday morning without saying goodbye." The words came out in a rush. "It's just that I'm a morning person, and you were sleeping so soundly, and I didn't want to wake you up."

He studied me like I was a puzzle he was trying to piece together.

"What did I do to get kicked out of my own bed and stuck sleeping on the couch?" he finally said, so casually that it was like he didn't care.

"What?" Of all the responses I'd braced myself for, that wasn't one of them.

"I woke up on the couch, and you were gone. So tell

me—what did I do to get kicked out of bed after we hooked up?"

I searched his expression for a hint that he was joking.

There was none.

Instead, he was staring down at me, his gaze locked on mine. The same intense energy buzzed between us that I'd felt when he'd showed me his magic on our walk to his dorm.

There was no way he didn't feel it, too.

"We didn't hook up…" I finally said.

Something that resembled shock crossed his face. "I know I have a reputation for being selective," he said. "But I find it hard to believe that I brought the hot new girl back to my room and we didn't hook up."

It was official—one of us was losing our mind.

And I knew it wasn't me.

"Do you have amnesia or something?" I finally asked.

He chuckled, like he found me mildly amusing. "Is that what they're calling being blackout drunk these days?"

Pain hit me like a knife in the heart, and I sucked a sharp breath of cold air into my lungs. "You weren't drunk."

"I was thoroughly smashed." He smirked and shook his head. "Which is a shame, because I would love to remember slamming Drake into that wall."

I clenched my fists to my side, angry now. "I might not party a lot, but I know what blackout drunk looks like," I said. "You weren't even tipsy. You were stone-cold sober."

I held his gaze, refusing to back down.

It was like we were in a staring contest, daring the other to break first. But neither of us were budging.

"You were checking me out in the first few rooms we went to," he said, and despite the cold, I felt my cheeks flush. "You saw how much I drank."

I pressed my lips together, since I couldn't deny it. "You said you have a high alcohol tolerance."

"I'm pretty damn talented at hiding it when I'm drunk," he said with what should have been an illegally attractive smirk. "But I can assure you—no one has a tolerance *that* high."

My feet felt like they were frozen to the ground, and my heart dropped. "You're saying you don't remember *anything?*"

"That's what blackout drunk means." He shrugged. "Sorry. And I appreciate your apology, but you should know that I'm not the relationship type." He paused for a moment and ran his eyes up and down my body, as if sizing me up. "If you want to keep hooking up, on the other hand…"

"I already told you—we didn't hook up," I snapped.

"And you should trust me to remember, since you were the one who was 'blackout drunk.'"

He looked at me like he pitied me. "Is this some half-hearted attempt to protect your reputation?"

I stared at him, speechless.

"Why are you doing this?" I finally asked, the words strained.

"Doing what?"

"Lying to me."

Something that I thought might be pain flashed across his eyes, but it was gone in a second.

"I'm sorry you don't like what I'm telling you," he said, controlled and steady. "But I don't think there's anything more to talk about here."

I narrowed my eyes. "You didn't say you're not lying to me."

The words hung between us, and I stood strong, daring him to contradict me.

"Summer," he said with what I could have sworn was sadness in his tone. "I don't know what you want from me here."

He might as well have twisted the knife that was already lodged in my heart.

"I want to see the person you showed me you were on Saturday night," I said.

His eyes hardened, and the emotional wall he'd constructed between us thickened. "This *is* who I am."

He ran his fingers through his hair, sounding exasperated now. "If you don't like it, that's fine. Most people don't. But you're clearly freezing, so I think it's time to go inside. You go back to your table, I'll go back to mine, and we don't have to talk to each other ever again. Sound good?"

No. It most definitely did *not* sound good.

The thought of never talking to him again made my heart hurt far more than it should, given that we barely knew each other.

But it was true—we barely knew each other. And if this was who Zane truly was, maybe not knowing each other was for the best.

He'd probably only been sweet to me Saturday night because he was trying to hook up with me. Alyssa had warned me that might be the case, but I'd refused to believe it.

Which had apparently been very, very naive.

"Sounds *great*," I said, and then I marched past him and into the dining hall, forcing myself not to glance over my shoulder and get another look at this person who was a ghost of who I'd believed him to be.

CHAPTER NINETEEN

I kept my back toward Zane all through lunch, and I could barely bring myself to eat.

Alyssa glanced at my nearly full plate. "We have elemental training this afternoon," she said. "You should eat more than half a slice of pizza. You'll want some energy to get through the class."

I picked up the half-eaten slice and forced myself to take a bite. It tasted like nothing. I might as well have been eating cardboard.

I put the slice back down in defeat, since my taste-buds had apparently gone on hiatus for the day.

Jamie pointed at my second slice. "If you're not eating that, can I have it?"

"Sure." I pushed the plate toward her, and she happily took it.

Alyssa and Jamie had spent most of lunch assuring

me that Zane was an asshole, and that I should be glad I didn't actually sleep with him. It didn't make me feel any better about Zane, but I *was* grateful that I had friends to support me.

"I don't know what I would have done these first few days without you guys," I said to them, although it was mainly to Alyssa.

I didn't know Jamie that well, but when she wasn't totally wasted, she did seem to have her heart in the right place. And it was nice to know someone who also grew up not knowing she was a witch.

"And I'm glad you were assigned to my suite," Alyssa said with a smile.

My watch buzzed, and I looked down at it.

A calendar alert.

Elemental air training at the gym in ten minutes.

I took out my phone and turned off my calendar alerts, since getting buzzed before every class was going to get annoying really quickly.

"What do we do in elemental training?" I asked them.

"Whatever our teacher wants us to work on," Jamie said. "Sometimes we'll spend a few classes in a row on one thing, and sometimes he'll mix it up. He likes to surprise us."

"I hope it's not archery again," Alyssa said. "I *hate* archery."

"The only time I've shot an arrow was when I

dressed as Katniss for Halloween," I said. "It didn't go well."

"What does 'didn't go well' mean?" she asked.

"It means I couldn't get the arrow to fly. The only thing I managed to hit was the ground."

Jamie winced.

"It was a *costume* arrow," Alyssa rushed to my rescue. "Of course it didn't work."

"Except my best friend managed to hit a tree on her first try," I said. "From the same distance."

"Oh." She frowned. "But that was before you got your magic. I'm sure you'll be fine."

"Right," I said, although I didn't truly believe it—especially since I'd yet to be able to use my magic on purpose.

"You'll be fine," Alyssa repeated, as if saying it again would make it true. "Anyway, we should head out. Mason hates when people are late."

"Mason?"

"Our teacher," she said. "He goes by his first name, since as air elementals, we're all equals in his eyes. Unless you're late. Then he'll give you a hard time for the entire class."

"Then let's definitely not be late," I said, and we got up to return our trays and head out of the dining hall.

I couldn't help it—I glanced over my shoulder to get a final glance at Zane.

But it didn't matter, because he was already gone.

There were thirteen of us in the class, and we gathered in the indoor basketball court. Jamie was already off to the side flirting with one of the guys I'd seen at the around the world party, but Alyssa stayed with me.

A man who looked a few years older than us strolled into the room, and everyone silenced. He had tan skin, silky brown hair tied into a man bun, and mysterious brown eyes. I'd never thought man buns were attractive, but he pulled it off flawlessly.

"Who's that?" I whispered to Alyssa.

"Mason," she said. "Our teacher."

"He doesn't look much older than us."

"Witches only started getting elemental abilities about seven years ago," she said, and then she shut her mouth, because Mason started walking toward us.

In his low hanging sweatpants and white ribbed tank top, he looked like a guy you'd see weightlifting in the gym.

He stopped when he was about six feet away. "I've had my magic for all seven years, and I was eighteen when I got it." He paused to size me up. "You must be Summer."

"The one and only," I said. "Unless you were

expecting another new student to drop in a week into the semester?"

"Funny." He smirked. "I like you."

"I doubt you'll be saying that once we start..." I glanced around the gym, but there were no hints about what we'd be doing for training. "Whatever we'll be doing today."

He crossed his arms and looked at me in challenge. "Swordplay."

I stopped breathing for a second. "With actual blades?"

He chuckled in amusement. "I want you trained—not dead," he said. "We use practice swords around here."

He snapped his fingers, wind whipped through the gym, and a long cart rolled out from an open door on the opposite side of the basketball court.

It held a row of wooden swords.

"Everyone—go grab a sword," he said. "Practice starts now."

The others jogged to the cart, and Alyssa and I followed. The wooden swords were identical replicas of each other, so I didn't have to worry about choosing a "good" one.

It was lighter than I'd expected, and it felt unnatural in my hand.

We returned to the center of the gym and faced

Mason. He also held a sword, although his was longer than ours.

"Pick a partner," he said, and I immediately turned to Alyssa.

"As if I'd pick anyone else?" she asked.

"I warned you how terrible I am at this stuff," I said. "If you end up losing an eye, I'm sorry in advance."

Mason turned to us. "Good pick," he said. "Alyssa, go to the side of the gym and fill Summer in on the basics."

Alyssa's eyes widened like a deer caught in the headlights.

"You're the best in the class," Mason told her. "You've got this."

I turned to Alyssa in surprise. It wasn't that I didn't think she'd be good at this stuff, but…

Who was I kidding? Alyssa was tiny, bouncy, and over-anxious. I totally hadn't thought she'd be good at this stuff, let alone the *best in the class.*

"I come from a long line of powerful witches." She shrugged. "But I've never been good at teaching."

"Now's a great time to try," Mason said, and then he winked at her. An actual, real-life wink. "Good luck."

He smirked at me again.

He was *definitely* expecting me to get my ass kicked.

Luckily, Alyssa didn't include any ass kicking in our session. Instead, she taught me how to stand to stay grounded and steady, and she showed me how to properly grip the handle of the sword. I had to mirror-image everything, since she was a righty, but we figured it out.

After covering the super-basics, she showed me a few moves and had me imitate them. She pointed out whenever our classmates made good moves while sparring, and she also explained their mistakes.

It didn't take long to see one of Alyssa's advantages in sword fighting—she was small and quick. She made it look like a choreographed dance.

I, on the other hand, wasn't as graceful.

Mason approached us when we only had ten minutes left of class.

"So," he said. "How's it been going over here?"

"Great!" Alyssa chirped, although from her tone, I could tell she only half-meant it.

"That good, huh?" He raised an eyebrow, then turned to me with his sword at the ready. "All right, Sunshine. Show me what you've got."

"Sunshine?" I repeated, rolling my eyes. "How original."

He came at me with his sword so quickly that he knocked mine out of my hand before I could blink. It flew behind me and smacked to the ground.

"Hey," I said. "I wasn't ready."

"Which means it was the best time for me to disarm

you," he said. "No opponent will ever wait until you're ready."

Alyssa stepped closer to me, looking like an angry pixie. "We didn't get that far," she said. "I taught her stances, grips, and *very* basic moves."

"I'm sure you did a great job," Mason said, and he turned to me again. "Get your sword."

I took a few steps back toward my sword, purposefully not turning away from him. For all I knew, he'd take it as an opportunity to attack again.

"Not like that," he said.

I stopped walking and looked at him in challenge. "I'm not turning my back to you."

"Smart." He nodded in approval. "But that's not what I meant."

I crossed my arms and waited for him to continue.

When it became clear that he wasn't going to say more, I asked, "Then what did you mean?"

"Come stand next to me."

I glanced at the spot next to him warily.

"Relax," he said. "I don't bite."

I straightened my shoulders and did as he asked, not letting my gaze leave his. I was *not* going to let him intimidate me, no matter how hard he tried.

The sword lay flat on the ground about ten feet ahead of us.

"Now what?" I asked him. "Do you want to race me?"

He took a few steps away from me and sized me up. "I want you to stay exactly where you are," he said. "And I want you to get your sword."

I suddenly became aware that the rest of the gym had quieted.

All my classmates were watching us.

My palms dampened with sweat.

"You want me to use magic," I realized.

"This is a training class for air elementals," he said. "I expect all my students to use magic. And you haven't used any for the entire time we've been here."

"How do you know that?"

"I've been watching."

Of course he had.

"Do you have eyes in the back of your head or something?" I asked, although I supposed if he did, the man bun would stop them from seeing much.

"I'm aware of my surroundings," he said. "Like you'll need to be in a fight."

I looked around at the class. Thanks to the fact that everyone in the school knew I had zero control over my magic, most of them looked amused—like I was their entertainment for the day. The only ones who looked at me with encouragement were Alyssa and Jamie.

I took a deep breath and focused on the sword, trying to calm the intense pounding of my heart.

I thought back to a few days ago in the testing room.

Focus on the color yellow, Kate had said. *Pull it up through your body and direct it through your palms.*

My palms were damp with sweat.

Hopefully sweat didn't block magic.

I held them up like I had in the testing room, feeling silly as I did it.

Yellow, I thought, and I imagined the color in my mind. I tried to feel around for it, since Alyssa had mentioned to me once that she did that.

I could picture it, but I couldn't *feel* it.

What would yellow feel like, anyway?

Sunshine? Warmth?

As hard as I tried, the only warmth I felt was the one crawling up my neck and cheeks at the thought of how much I was going to embarrass myself in front of everyone watching.

I glanced at Mason for direction, but he just stood there smirking.

Ugh.

Irritation coursed through me. But I couldn't just stand there doing nothing.

Since I was out of any other options, I tried to send the frustration through my palms, imagining wind strong enough to blow the sword toward me.

The basketball hoops creaked.

But the sword stayed where it was.

"Enough," Mason said, and wind blew toward us, the sword flying to him. Its handle smacked into his palm like he was a Jedi using the Force. He wrapped his fingers around it, his eyes not leaving mine, and announced, "Class dismissed."

Then he turned away and didn't look at me again.

CHAPTER TWENTY

After swordplay, we went to the massive fitness center, where we had our asses handed to us in a high intensity interval training class by an instructor named Kayla.

Well, *I* had my ass handed to me. The others had been doing this type of training for months, so they weren't huffing, puffing, red-faced messes like I was. But at least they were also all sweating.

Alyssa and I took turns in the shower when we got back, then headed down to the common room to grab dinner. It was taco night, and I was famished after that intense workout. We joined Jamie and the guy she was talking to in the gym today—Greg—at a table in the corner. Most of the air students liked to go to the dining hall for dinner—one of the benefits of being put in the most social dorm on campus—so we had the common room nearly to ourselves.

"Mason was crazy harsh on you in class today," Jamie said when Alyssa and I sat down.

"You mean he's not like that with every student?" I asked.

"Oh, he is," Greg said. "He picks on a different student each week. He gets off on it or something."

"But asking a total newbie to do something that the highest level witches can barely do?" Jamie said. "I've never seen him do *that*."

"You mean you all can't call swords into your hands like Jedis using the Force?" I asked.

"Like what?" Jamie asked.

"The Force," I said slowly. "From *Star Wars*."

"Haven't seen it."

Greg looked at Jamie like she was an alien. "You haven't seen *Star Wars*?"

"Um… no."

"We're gonna have to fix that," he declared. "I can't go around with a girl who hasn't seen *Star Wars*."

I looked back and forth between them in confusion. "Are you two dating?"

"We're hanging out," Jamie said quickly.

"I thought you had a boyfriend."

"We broke up."

"When?"

"Yesterday." She shrugged like it was no big deal. "Anyway, back to Mason. He's hot, isn't he?"

"He's an asshole," I said.

She waggled her eyebrows. "Those are always the hottest ones."

My thoughts immediately went to Zane, with his ice-blue eyes that cut through my soul. Because when it came to the assholes I'd dealt with today, my confrontation outside the dining hall with Zane took the cake.

I took a sip of my soda to clear my thoughts.

"The answer to your question is no," Alyssa said. "No one in our class could call their sword into their hand like Mason did today. That's some seriously high-level magic."

"So why did he ask *me* to do it?"

"Like you said, he's an asshole," Jamie said. "He was probably trying to get a rise out of you."

"Well, he succeeded." I huffed, then took an angry bite of my taco.

"You'll get the hang of it." Alyssa stood up, grabbed a stack of napkins from the buffet, and placed them on top of the empty table next to us. "Try using your magic to blow these to the floor."

"Can't you see that I'm drowning my misery in my food?" I took another huge bite for emphasis.

"Fine," she said. "Finish your dinner, then try."

I felt like a child being scolded, but I didn't care. I just wanted to be back at Hollins, in my apartment with Lara, going to normal classes and hanging out in the off-student campus lounge during the day. I never thought I'd miss that place—it was a dump compared to everything at the academy—but right now, I didn't care.

I'd even take bully sorority girls over bully teachers. I'd also take guys who ignored me over guys who were beyond sweet to me, then acted like they didn't know me two days later.

Guys whose names started with a Z, ended with an E, and rhymed with "pain."

"Finished?" Alyssa asked after I put down the final half of my fourth taco in defeat.

"I thought you said you weren't a teacher?" I asked.

"I'm not," she said. "But I'm your friend, and I want to help you learn how to use your magic."

"And she can't do that when you're throwing yourself a Tex-Mex pity party," Jamie added.

"I wasn't throwing a pity party."

"You were sulking into your tacos," she said. "You were *totally* throwing a pity party."

"We all need pity parties sometimes," Alyssa said cheerfully. "But right now, you need to learn how to harness your magic. Unless you want Mason to keep picking on you?"

"Totally understandable if you do," Jamie said. "He's hot when he gets like that."

Greg pressed his lips together in what looked like jealousy.

Jamie didn't notice.

I rotated in my chair and looked at the pile of napkins. There were about ten of them. "What do I need to do?" I asked.

"Let's start with this," Alyssa said. "What *have* you been doing?"

"I've been doing what Kate told me to—picturing the color yellow, reaching inside myself for my magic, and trying to push it out of my palms."

"And what do you feel when you reach inside yourself?"

"Nothing," I said, frustrated again. "Absolutely nothing."

She paused to think.

"Maybe you're putting too much pressure on yourself," she said. "You need to relax."

"How?"

"Easy." She smiled. "You should have some wine."

"Spoken like a true descendent of Dionysus," Greg said.

"Is alcohol your answer to everything?" I chuckled.

"Not *everything*," she said. "But it can help a lot of things. Like with relaxing. So, which do you prefer—red or white?"

"White," I said without hesitation. "Red makes me tired and headachy."

Alyssa frowned, as if disliking any type of wine was a personal insult. "What type of white?"

"I don't know." I shrugged. "They all kind of taste the same?"

She crossed her arms in irritation. "There's pinot grigio, chardonnay, sauvig—"

"I'll get it." Jamie stood up, left the common room, then returned quickly with a bottle of white wine. She presented it ostentatiously to Alyssa, as if we were at an expensive steakhouse ready to be served. "Will this one do?"

"It's a screw top." She scrunched her nose in distaste. "But I don't feel like going all the way upstairs to get one of mine, so fine. Let's go for it."

Greg got the plastic cups, and Jamie poured the wine evenly between the four of us.

Alyssa held her cup up in a toast. "To mastering magic," she said.

"To not getting my ass kicked again," I added.

We clinked our cups together and started to drink and chat. Jamie was more than happy to continue to fill me in on the others at the school—and any gossip she knew about them.

"Sorry about Zane," she eventually said. "Guys can be such idiots sometimes. Well, most of the time."

"Hey!" Greg gave her a playful punch, but she gave me an exasperated smile and didn't refute her statement.

"It's fine," I said, even though it wasn't. "Actually, it's for the best. I need to learn how to use my magic. I don't need a guy distracting me from that."

"Speaking of." Alyssa straightened, then placed her empty cup down on the table. "How much of that have you finished?"

I glanced down into my cup. There was only a bit of wine left.

I lifted it to my lips and chugged it.

When I finished it off, the tingly feeling of being slightly tipsy buzzed in my head.

"Hey!" Alyssa said. "Wine isn't meant to be chugged."

"It was a five-dollar screw top." Jamie rolled her eyes. "Chill."

"*Anyway.*" Alyssa narrowed her eyes at Jamie, then turned to me. "Now that you're appropriately relaxed, try to use your magic."

"All right." I took a deep breath and focused on the pile of napkins.

"Think about the color yellow," Alyssa reminded me.

"I know."

As if I could forget?

I tried my absolute hardest to picture yellow in my

mind, then tried to push it out through my palms to create wind to blow the napkins off the table.

Nothing happened.

"Visualize pulling the color inside yourself," Alyssa said. "Feel it in the air, like a breeze against your skin, and soak it in."

I nodded, closed my eyes to help me visualize, and reached out with my mind.

The air remained still.

"Ugh." I lowered my hands in frustration. "This isn't working."

Greg knocked the screw top that had been next to him on the table to the floor, as if he was as frustrated as I was.

"Huh." He picked it up and threw it into the trash can across the room. A slight breeze stirred in the air, and he made a perfect shot.

"Show off," Jamie said.

"I know you like it when I show off." He winked.

Jamie pointed her palm toward the stack of napkins, then effortlessly created enough of a breeze to send them fluttering off the table and onto the floor.

Greg rolled his eyes at her. "Elemental Magic 101."

Jamie and Alyssa glared at him.

He froze, then looked at me. "Sorry," he said quickly. "I didn't mean it like that."

"You did," I said. "But you're not wrong. I suck at using my magic."

"It's a learning curve," Alyssa said. "You'll get it."

"How long did it take you to be able to do something like that?"

She pressed her lips together.

Jamie and Greg didn't say anything, either.

"You could do it from day one," I realized. "It was basically the same thing as the paper Kate wanted me to blow off the table in the test."

"Everyone's different," she said. "You were able to blow those crystals back around to hit that sorority girl. Your magic is there. You must just have a mental block stopping you from accessing it."

"You could always find a guy to help you relieve some of that stress." Jamie leaned forward and tossed her braids over her shoulder. "I can make some recommendations. Just let me know your type."

Zane was the first thought that crossed my mind.

But I held my tongue.

"Summer's not a descendent of Zeus," Alyssa said in irritation.

"We don't know what she is," Jamie said. "She hasn't been claimed."

"I'm right here," I said. "And random hookups aren't my thing. Neither is getting wasted." I glanced at Alyssa apologetically. "Sorry."

"We all deal with stress differently," she said. "No offense taken."

"Cool."

Greg took a moment to study me. "So if you don't seem like a descendent of Zeus or Dionysus, then you must be related to Hermes. Welcome to the cool kids' club."

"Aren't descendants of Hermes usually athletic?" I asked.

"We are."

"Then I promise you—I'm *not* a descendent of Hermes."

"Question," Jamie said, and she continued before I could tell her to go on. "Are you a virgin?"

"What?" I said, even though I'd clearly heard her. "Why does that matter?"

"Because you don't like sports, and you don't like partying. But you can't dislike something you've never tried."

I played with the tips of my fingers, then dropped my hand to my side.

Ever since Zane had pointed out that he'd noticed my fidgeting, I'd become infinitely more aware of it.

"You *are* a virgin." Jamie brightened, like she'd figured out a secret of the universe. "Aren't you?"

"I am," I said, since it wasn't anything to be ashamed of. I'd just been caught off-guard by how casually she'd asked. "And that's not changing until I meet the right guy."

Again, Zane's frustratingly perfect face flashed through my mind.

Oh my God.

He really needed to *stop* invading my thoughts.

"No worries," she said. "Just figured it couldn't hurt to ask."

Alyssa got up and gathered the napkins. "Want to try again?" she asked.

"Not right now," I said. "I have some reading to catch up on. But thanks."

"Reading for what?"

"For art history. And English. And quantitative reasoning. Which I'm also going to need help with, because my brain wasn't built for math."

"You sound more like an earth elemental than an air elemental," Greg said. "I think they're the only ones who do all their assigned reading."

"So I've heard," I said, and then I cleaned up my stuff, said goodnight to the three of them, and headed back up to my room.

CHAPTER TWENTY-ONE

Two more days passed, and Zane and I successfully avoided looking at each other during lunch for both of them.

Sort of.

I always glanced his way when I walked into the dining hall, then forced myself to look away when he didn't notice my presence.

But it was okay. I was fine.

Well, not emotionally fine. But I could bury that in something I'd always excelled in—regular academic classes.

It hadn't taken me long to catch up on them. My academic teachers already loved me as much as they had at Hollins, and the earth elementals had welcomed me to sit with them in the front rows of the classrooms. They were shy, but when I was near them,

I felt comfortable in a way that I never felt in the air dorm.

Still, they were wary around me, which served as a reminder that while I cared about academics, I wasn't one of them.

I *wished* I were one of them.

My afternoon witchy classes on Tuesday—History of Magic and Introduction to Greek Mythology—went well. My History of Magic professor, a kind man named Mr. Faulkner, had even printed me out some extra reading material to help me catch up.

But today was Wednesday, which meant another afternoon magic training class with Mason.

The pit of dread that I'd woken up with that morning grew as I walked with Alyssa and Jamie to the gym.

"It'll probably be sword fighting again," Jamie said. "Mason *loves* his sword."

"*You* love his sword," I joked, since I was quickly learning how often Jamie made sexual references, and how she took no offense when teased back.

She stuck her tongue out. "I'd play with his sword any day."

"What happened with Greg?" Alyssa asked.

"Topher helped me with some homework last night." She shrugged at the mention of the earth elemental she'd told me was her boyfriend at the around the world party. "Greg wasn't happy about it."

I understood why, but I kept my mouth shut. Jamie's love life was her problem. Well, it was Greg and Topher's problem, since Jamie seemed unfazed by jumping back and forth between the two of them.

At least Jamie's preoccupation with them had diverted her from trying to find me a random guy to hook up with.

When we entered the gym, there were five large archery targets set up on the far side of the basketball court, and bows and arrows across from them. The targets were the typical colored foam ones propped up with four metal legs.

"Archery!" Jamie's eyes lit up. "My favorite."

"I thought swordplay was your favorite?" I asked.

"All sports are my favorite."

With that, she hurried over to inspect the bows and arrows, feeling each one to presumably pick one she liked best.

There were a few other students already sitting on the bleachers, holding bows they'd chosen. Off to the side, Mason stood chatting with Nicole.

Nicole smiled when she saw me, and she jogged over to where Alyssa and I were standing. She had a bow strapped onto her back, and it moved like it was a part of her.

"Hey!" she said once she'd joined us. "Sorry I haven't checked in. How's it been going with your classes?"

"The others are great," I said, and then I glanced at Mason, who was clearly trying to listen in on our conversation from across the room. "This one... not so much."

"You'll get there," she said encouragingly.

"You wouldn't be saying that if you saw my last few attempts." I chuckled to try making a joke of it, but my frustration definitely came through.

"You're doing great," Alyssa said, although it sounded forced. She tacked on a smile to be more convincing.

I shrugged, since I definitely *wasn't* doing great.

"What're you doing here?" I asked Nicole. "Don't you have your own classes?"

"Archery is my specialty." She grinned. "I'm helping out today."

"Mason gave up on me that quickly?"

Right after I finished the sentence, the teacher in question came strolling up to us.

"Mason wants to help you as much as possible," he said, and I rolled my eyes, since he *would* talk about himself in the third person.

My heart dropped, and I looked back at Nicole. "So you're here because of how much I suck at using my magic?"

"No." She glared at Mason. "My bio-dad—Apollo—is the god of archery, amongst other things. I pop by sometimes during archery lessons to give advice on technique."

I glanced at Alyssa, and she gave me a tiny nod to let me know that Nicole was telling the truth.

"I'm gonna need as much advice as possible," I said. "You should have seen what happened when I dressed as Katniss for Halloween last year."

"I'm sure it wasn't *that* bad," Nicole said.

"It was definitely that bad."

"It can't get much worse than your swordplay," Mason said, and I glared at him, like Nicole had just done. "Now—choose a bow, and let's get started."

<hr />

My "skills" in archery were as terrible as I'd warned they'd be.

The other students weren't hitting back-to-back bullseyes or anything—the only one who could do that was Nicole—but at least they hit part of the target most of the time.

My arrows always came up short.

Even Nicole seemed frustrated with me by the end of class.

"Ground yourself and pull back on the bow as steadily as you can," she said what she'd been repeating over and over again. "Focus on the bullseye. Then breathe out, tune into your magic, and let the arrow fly."

It was the "tune into your magic" part that I struggled with the most. Although the fact that I had basically no upper arm strength was coming in a close second.

Come on, magic, I thought to myself, since by this point, I was at a loss for how to purposefully "tune into" it. *Do your thing.*

I closed my eyes and took a deep breath, trying to imagine magic filling me, all the way out to my fingers and toes.

I could have sworn I felt a tingle.

Figuring that was good enough, I opened my eyes, stared at the bullseye, and released my hold on the string of the bow.

The arrow landed ten feet short of the target.

I cursed and threw the bow to my feet in a wave of frustration.

But the crash that followed was more than the bow hitting the floor.

It was the *clang* of metal on wood as the targets fell backward, their stands hitting the ground.

Everyone silenced and stared at the fallen targets.

The only one who wasn't focused on the targets was Nicole. She was looking straight at me.

"Did you do that?" she asked.

"I don't know," I said. "I was frustrated, and then..."

I glanced at the fallen targets, since there was no need to explain further.

But how could I have done that? Knocking over heavy objects—and so many of them at once—was way more advanced than anything I should be able to do.

"There was no wind," Mason's voice boomed through the gym.

"What?" I asked.

"Whenever air elementals use our magic, it's always accompanied by at least a breeze," he said. "But when those targets fell backward, the air was still."

"I understood that part," I said. "But what does that *mean?*"

He pressed his lips together, perplexed. "I have no idea," he admitted, and then he looked to some of the guys standing across the gym. "Prop one of the targets back up."

Greg and one of the other guys did as he'd asked.

Mason's eyes were like laser beams boring through me. "Do it again."

The other students remained silent. Which was eerie, given how chatty the air elementals usually were.

"All right." I swallowed, rotated to face the target, and stared at it.

I did this a minute ago. There was no reason I shouldn't be able to do it again.

Minus the fact that all eyes were on me. The pressure

was like a physical thing in the air that I could reach out and touch. It was like I was on stage performing for an audience, and I'd never been much of a theatre kid.

"You've got this," Alyssa said, and I gave her a small smile, grateful for her encouragement.

She was standing next to Nicole, who was watching me carefully, sizing me up.

My heart felt like it was pounding a million beats per minute, and my lungs tightened so much that I couldn't pull in a deep breath. Sweat dampened my palms.

"What are you waiting for?" Mason challenged. "Show us what you've got."

I held my palms out toward the target, my mind spinning.

Magic. Do your thing, I thought, since that was what I did last time.

Nothing happened.

Anxiety rushed through me, and the corners of my vision blurred.

"This isn't working." I lowered my arms back to my sides. "I don't know what knocked all the targets down before, but it wasn't me."

Mason narrowed his eyes, and everyone remained silent. "Pick your bow back up," he said, and then he looked around at the others in the gym. "The rest of you —stop standing around. We're here to practice, so get your lazy selves back to work."

CHAPTER TWENTY-TWO

I was sitting at my desk struggling with some math problems in my Quantitative Reasoning textbook when Alyssa burst into my room, holding a thin red book in her hand.

I accidentally hit a random button on my calculator, destroying the progress I'd been making on the equation.

"What's up?" I tried not to sound annoyed as I tapped the all-clear button so I could start over again.

"I have an idea," she said.

"About…?"

"It was you who knocked those targets over in archery."

"You heard Mason," I said. "There was no wind. It couldn't have been me."

"There was also no wind when you knocked that bottle cap off the table Monday night," she said.

I placed my pencil down. "When I what?"

"Greg thought he knocked that bottle cap off the table. But I saw it happen. His elbow was near the cap, but he never actually touched it."

"Are you saying it fell off the table on its own?"

"No. It fell off the table while you were trying to use your magic to blow the napkins off the other table."

"But my palms weren't facing the bottle cap."

"They weren't facing the targets either." She shrugged. "But you still knocked them over."

"I didn't," I said, wishing she'd stop so I could get back to my homework.

"You were frustrated because you were having a tough time with archery," she said. "Just like how you were frustrated with the napkins, and with that sorority girl at your old school."

"I wasn't 'frustrated' with Courtney," I said. "I was *enraged.*"

"Rightly so," she said. "My point is that you're only able to use your magic when you're angry. And when you do, you have no control over what you're doing with it."

"You're still assuming I knocked that bottle cap off the table, and that I knocked down those targets."

"I'm not 'assuming,'" she said. "I'm observing a pattern. And if my observation is correct—which I think it is—then you need to learn how to use your magic when you're not angry."

"I totally agree," I said, and I motioned to the textbook open in front of me. "But this homework is due tomorrow, and at this rate, I'm going to be up all night working on it."

"You can copy mine," she said simply.

"I'm not copying your homework," I said, appalled.

"It'll be fine," she said, continuing before I could disagree again. "The thing I want to try is more important. And it has to be done on the new moon, which is tonight."

At the mention of the new moon, I thought of my mom. She liked to gather water from the stream near our house on the nights of the new and full moons. We'd think about our intentions for the next two weeks, and leave the water bottles outside overnight. We'd drink the water the next morning, so the intentions would become part of us.

I needed to call her soon. I'd been avoiding talking to her because the thought of how much lying I'd need to do made my stomach roll, but I couldn't put it off forever.

"What are you thinking about?" Alyssa asked.

I glanced at the red book, not wanting to talk about my mom right now. "What's this 'thing' you want to try?" I asked instead.

She held up the book so the cover faced me. Most of it was red, but there was a small parchment-colored rectangle in the center with the title *The Good Spell Book* on the front. There were some other words beneath it, but she was standing too far away for me to make them out.

"It's time to delve into some spell magic," she said, and then she sat cross-legged on the rug. "Come sit with me."

"No one's mentioned spell magic yet," I said.

"That's because it's pagan magic, and it steps into some gray areas," she said. "But don't worry about it— my mom's totally practiced in this kind of magic, and she's been working with me on it for years. I know what I'm doing. And I found something in this book that will help you."

I couldn't deny it—I was intrigued.

So I closed my textbook over my pencil to hold my place, got out of my chair, and sat across from Alyssa. She had a mischievous glint in her eyes, and excitement for whatever we were about to do rushed through me.

Now that I was closer to the book, I could make out the writing below the main title. *Love Charms, Candle Spells, and Other Practical Sorcery*. There were three thin gold ribbons attached to the top to mark the pages.

"Are we allowed to do this?" I asked. "I don't want to

get locked into whatever prison you all must have for witches."

"Most of these spells aren't dark magic, so they won't hurt anyone," she said. "And I've found one to help you heal your magic. So are you in, or not?"

"I'm in."

"Good." She nodded in approval. "I'll get the materials. Stay here."

She went into her room, and I looked at the book. It was small and unassuming. But I didn't touch it—I didn't want it to electric shock me or something.

I wondered what type of love spells were in there…

Alyssa quickly returned with a small woven basket full of materials. She sat down, set it beside us, and started pulling out crystals, candles, and little bottles. Once empty, she turned the basket upside-down and placed it between us. It was only a few inches high.

"This is our altar," she declared.

"A basket can be an altar?" I didn't know much about magic, but that seemed pretty unofficial.

"We're the witches," she said mischievously. "We make the rules."

A chill of excitement ran up my spine.

She picked up a white ceramic object that was a bit larger than a thimble and set it in the center of the altar. A gold pentagram was etched on its side.

Next, she picked up a thin, white candle that was

about three inches tall and placed it inside the white ceramic object, which was apparently a candle holder.

"You need to anoint the candle," she declared, handing me a small glass bottle.

"Essential oil," I said.

"How'd you know that?"

"My mom uses them in diffusers around our house."

"Interesting." She studied me for a moment, then she pointed at the bottle. "This is Juniper Berry. It attracts empowerment."

"Cool." I glanced back and forth between the bottle and the candle. "How do I 'anoint' the candle?"

"Put a few drops of oil in your palms. Then pick up the candle, rub the oil on as much of it as you can, and put the candle back in the holder. Make sure to rub the oil toward you, since you're trying to bring the ability to control your magic inside you."

She made it sound so simple.

Trying not to overthink it, I uncapped the vial and emptied a few drops of the sweet-smelling oil onto my palm. Then I picked up the candle and rubbed it between my hands in an attempt to coat as much of it as possible. Once finished, I placed the candle back into its holder, pressed it down to make sure it was secure, and brought my palms up to my face to inhale the sweet oil, letting the scent travel through me.

"You're a natural." Alyssa took a few drops onto her

palms and inhaled it as well. Then she handed me a matchbook. "Now, light the candle."

It took me three tries with three different matches, but eventually I got a spark and was able to light the candle. The three used matches were now in a small copper bowl that also had a pentagram on it, although this pentagram had two crescent moons on its sides.

"Next, the crystals." Alyssa picked up a green one and placed it on her side of the candle. "Aventurine to the north, to represent the element of earth," she said, and then she continued clockwise. Blue lapis to the east to represent water, red agate to the south to represent fire, and yellow citrine to the west to represent air.

I remained silent as I watched, as if saying anything would break the energy crackling in the air.

She cast her eyes downward "I invite Hecate into our circle, to protect our energy," she said mystically.

I looked down as well, unsure what else to do.

The flame burned higher, and goosebumps prickled along my arms, as if some sort of spiritual force had entered the room. But it didn't feel ghostlike or eerie. It felt protective, like warm energy blanketing my skin.

"The circle is ready," Alyssa declared.

"Great." I didn't know what else to say, since this all felt foreign to me. "Who's Hecate?"

"The Greek goddess of witchcraft," she said. "She's not one of the Olympians, so no one at the academy is descended from her. She's actually not talked about much at all, which I've always found strange, since all of us are witches. But my mom's always said she's there in the background, ready to help those of us who seek her."

"Got it," I said, adding it to the growing list of new information I'd been compiling in my mind ever since arriving at Elementals Academy.

"Anyway," she continued, and she picked up a green leaf and a gold pen, handing them to me. "This is a bay leaf and a pen that's never been used. Write your intention on the leaf, then burn the leaf in the flame and drop it into our offering bowl."

I placed the bay leaf in front of me on the altar, took the pen, and wrote "control my magic" on the leaf. Then I picked up the leaf, touched the tip of it to the flame, and dropped it inside the copper offering bowl. It continued to burn, the flame traveling downward to its base.

Alyssa thrust a clear jagged crystal toward me. "Hold this," she instructed, and I wrapped my palm around it.

Another wave of warm energy passed through me, and I stared at the singed bay leaf, watching the fire burn through it.

The clear crystal pulsed in my hand.

And then the four crystals around the candle rose into the air, until they were floating at the same height as the candle.

CHAPTER TWENTY-THREE

A lyssa gasped, her eyes wide as she stared at the crystals.

"I'm not doing that," she said slowly.

"I know you're not," I said. "Because I am."

I looked at the stones and *nudged* them with my mind.

They slowly started rotating clockwise around the candle. The candle's flame burned steady and straight.

There was no breeze.

Alyssa and I watched the stones in wonder.

Go back down, I thought to them, and they floated back down onto the altar.

"Your magic must be insanely strong to move them without a breeze," she said once the crystals were settled. "Like you're controlling the air on a molecular level."

"I didn't know you liked science."

"I don't." She smiled. "Did it sound like I knew what I was talking about?"

"Totally," I said. "But I don't feel like I'm connecting with the air. I feel like I'm connecting with the stones."

"Hm." She frowned. "Interesting."

"It's weird, isn't it?"

"I have no idea." She shrugged. "But you controlled your magic. Isn't that what counts?"

"It is," I said, and then my watch started buzzing. I glanced down at the screen. "My mom's calling." Panic fluttered through me, since I hadn't talked to her since coming to the academy. "I need to pick up."

"Sure," Alyssa said. "I'll come back for my stuff later."

She left through our shared bathroom, and I hurried to my bed to accept the FaceTime call.

I swallowed down tears at the sight of my mom's dark hair and warm, deep blue eyes. Other than our eye color, she looked so much like me that people were always surprised to find out I was adopted.

I plastered on what I hoped was a casual, relaxed smile. "What's up?" I asked.

"Just checking in to see how you're adjusting to your new school," she said calmly. "I know it has to be quite the change."

Understatement of the year.

"It's cold," I said the first non-specific thing that came to mind.

"Sounds like you'll get good use of that new jacket and boots."

"For sure." I had no idea how she thought I got my new winter gear, but I didn't want to keep talking about it. "My suitemate's nice," I said instead.

"That's great!" she said. "What's her name?"

"Alyssa."

"Where's she from?"

"Somewhere near Boston," I said, since I couldn't remember the exact name of the town. "We're in all the same classes together."

"I'm really glad to hear you're already making friends," she said. "I know you must miss Lara a lot."

"Yeah," I said, although the truth was that I'd had so much going on that I hadn't thought about Lara much since getting there.

"Your classes are good?"

My first thought was of my air elemental training class, which was *far* from going well. But I couldn't talk to my mom about that.

I wasn't used to hiding things from her. And I didn't like it.

"Hey, I have a bunch of work I have to get done before tomorrow," I said quickly, glancing at my math textbook on the desk. "Let's catch up another day?"

"Sounds good," she said. "And remember—this school is a great opportunity for you. I know it must feel foreign and strange, but you're where you're meant to be. Okay?"

What on Earth had the Elders told her about the academy? I'd ask her, but I didn't want to sound suspicious. So I made a mental note to ask Nicole about it soon.

"Sure," I said. "Thanks. Talk soon."

"Good luck on that homework," she said, and then I pressed the button to end the call, feeling instant relief that the pressure to lie was gone.

I walked over to my desk and settled in to start tackling the math problem I'd started before, but couldn't focus.

My eyes kept wandering to the candle burning on the altar, and the red spell book beside it. The flame called to me, like it was telling me that the circle we'd created for the ceremony was still open to explore. And I felt inexplicably drawn to the book.

Maybe if I took a short break to look through it, I'd be able to focus on my homework.

Come to me, I thought to the book, trying to will it to lift off the ground and float over to my desk.

Nothing happened.

I tried again, trying to connect with the book like I'd connected with the stones. But still, nothing.

So I grudgingly got up, sat cross-legged in front of the altar, and opened the book.

The first section was the one about love spells, and I flipped through the pages to see what they were.

To win the heart of the one you love.
To attract the one you love.
To find a lover.
To strengthen attraction.

As I read through them, my thoughts went to Zane and how harsh he'd been at lunch on Monday. Thinking about it hurt. Because despite what he'd said about not remembering the night of the party, I truly believed he was lying. *Why* he would lie was beyond me, but it was my gut instinct.

I stopped flipping the pages when I came across a spell that spoke to me.

To get a loving response.

It required a quartz crystal ball, and a photo of the person I was trying to reach.

I had neither of those things. And Zane didn't have any social media accounts—I'd checked already—so using a digital photo wasn't an option.

I flipped to the next page to see what other spells there were… and then there was a knock on the door that led to the bathroom.

I slammed the book shut, and the crystals on the altar jumped a bit, too.

"Come in!" I said, my voice higher than normal.

Alyssa stepped inside—she was now wearing purple pajamas—and she looked suspiciously at the spell book in my lap. "I was getting ready for bed and didn't hear any talking, so I figured you were off the phone," she said. "What spell were you looking for?"

"Nothing in particular," I said quickly. "Just browsing."

She walked over and sat across from me, her eyes more serious than ever. "I know we've only known each other for less than a week, but I can already tell when you're lying."

"Fine." I figured it wouldn't hurt to be honest with her, no matter how embarrassing the answer was. And I truly wanted to be friends with her. Which meant telling her the truth. "I was looking at love spells."

She tilted her head, curious. "What did you find?"

"Let me start off by saying I think Zane was lying when he told me he was too drunk to remember

Saturday night," I said. "I want to know what's really going on with him, and confronting him obviously didn't work out. So I found this."

I flipped back to the previous page and laid the book open between us.

She studied it for a few seconds, then looked back up to me. "What sort of response do you want to get from him?"

"I want him to tell me he was lying."

"And if he wasn't lying?"

"I'm pretty sure he was."

Alyssa picked up the spell book, used one of the thin ribbons to mark the page, then shut it.

"Here's the thing about spells," she said seriously. "Your intention matters. From what you just told me, your intention is to get the response that *you* want to hear. Which means you're not in the right headspace to cast this spell."

"What's the 'right headspace'?"

She chewed her lower lip as she thought. "Something along the lines of wanting him to feel comfortable communicating with you about what happened that night, no matter what that truth might be."

"All right," I said. "Let's do it that way. Any chance you have a quartz crystal ball and a photo of him?"

"I have a rose quartz sphere, which is perfect for love spells," she said. "I don't have a photo of him. But either way, given what you just told me, this isn't the right time to perform this spell."

"Sounds like I'll have to secretly snap a photo of him so we can do this spell another day," I said, and then I paused, thinking about what I'd just said. "Wait. That sounded creepy."

"Magic can be creepy sometimes." She shrugged. "But what happened to that stuff you told me this morning about needing to forget about guys so you can focus on school?"

I glanced guiltily at my math textbook, which was open to the same page it had been on when Alyssa had first come into my room. "You're right," I said. "School needs to be my priority. And I guess if Zane truly wants to say something to me, he'll find a way to say it, whether I do this spell or not."

"Absolutely," she agreed, and she motioned to the altar. "I'm going to take all this stuff. Except for the candle, because I want you to leave it on your nightstand and let it burn out naturally."

"I can do that."

She placed the candle on my nightstand, then started packing the other materials into the basket.

"Are you sure you don't want to copy my homework?" she asked once she was done. "It's getting late..."

"I'm sure," I said. "Anyway, I think I've got it figured

out. All I need now is to practice. And I don't need a lot of sleep—remember?"

"I'm so jealous about that, by the way." She stood up and headed toward the door. "Good luck!"

"Thanks," I said. "And thanks for helping me out tonight. I needed it."

"That's what friends are for," she said, and then she left me alone to finish tackling my math homework, which was only slightly less frustrating than learning how to master my magic.

CHAPTER TWENTY-FOUR

M y gaze naturally went to Zane's table when I walked into the dining hall with Alyssa and Jamie the next day.

He wasn't there.

Which meant if I got through the cafeteria line quickly enough, I could sit down at my table with my back toward his, and not have to worry about accidentally seeing him until it was time to leave.

I'd also have to make sure my back was toward the entrance, so I didn't see him when he came in. And I couldn't look at the cafeteria line, either.

Oh my God.

There was something wrong with me. I should *not* be so anxious about all of this. Zane was just a guy—and not just *any* guy, but one who'd been a total asshole to me. He didn't deserve all the space in my mind that I was giving him.

Maybe there was a spell I could do to force myself to stop thinking about him?

I decided on the seat looking out the window to the lake, and the three of us started chatting about regular things—mainly, Jamie's love life. There was another guy thrown into the mix now. A fire elemental named Shane. Or Shawn. Something like that.

"Why not just have a boyfriend from each element?" I joked. "Find one in the water dorm, and you'll be set."

"You mean like a reverse harem?"

"Sure."

"Trust me—I've thought about it," she said. "But they've made it more than clear that they wouldn't be down for that. Thus, the constant struggle of having to choose." She sighed and took a dramatic bite of her French fry.

"Um, Summer?" Alyssa said, her pizza midway to her mouth. "I think you-know-who is coming our way..."

There was only one person she could mean, and panic seized me when I turned around and saw Zane casually walking to the only open seat at our four-top table—the one between me and Jamie. He was carrying his cafeteria tray, and his ice-blue eyes locked on mine.

The corner of his sinfully delicious-looking lips curved up slightly in amusement.

"Is someone sitting here?" he asked calmy, as if him joining another table was a totally normal occurrence.

I stared up at him, stunned. "You want to sit with us?" I finally asked.

"That's why I came over here."

Alyssa and Jamie were silent, clearly leaving the decision to me.

I had no idea what to do. Because why did he want to sit with us? What was he up to? Was he toying with me? Again?

I couldn't focus on any of my thoughts. But I needed to say something.

Now.

"Sure." I hoped I sounded calmer than I felt, given that every nerve in my body had been zapped into overdrive. "That seat's empty."

He slid into the chair and placed his tray down in front of him. He had four burger patties stacked on top of each other—no bun, no cheese, and no sides.

"You like meat," I said, and then I internally cringed.

Out of everything I could have said, *that* was the first thing that had come out of my mouth?

My cheeks heated, and I couldn't bring myself to look him in the eyes.

Jamie's expression was pained.

Maybe I needed to get advice from her tonight about how to not act like a total moron around guys.

"I do." He removed his utensils from his napkin, then started eating the patties with a fork and knife. "How have your classes been going?"

"Are you drunk or something?"

He paused midway through cutting his burger, as if I'd struck a nerve. "It's the middle of the day," he said. "And I'm not a descendent of Dionysus."

"Hey," Alyssa cut in. "I don't go to classes drunk."

"Maybe not." He shrugged. "But most of you have at some point or another."

Alyssa frowned, then took a sip of her Coke, not denying it.

"Vera's glaring at us like she wants to throw us in the lake and drown us," Jamie finally said.

I rotated slightly to see what she was talking about.

Sure enough, Vera was as still as a statue, and she was staring at me like she wanted to turn me to ice and shatter me to pieces. Her hair was perfectly curled, and her makeup was flawless, down to the cat-eye wings on her lids.

Chills ran down my spine at her sharp gaze.

Zane glared back at Vera and got in a staring contest with her until she lowered her eyes. "She's territorial," he said, turning back around to face the table. "Ignore her. I've got her handled."

"You're talking about her like she's some sort of pet," I said.

"Or like she's your girlfriend," Jamie added.

"She's *not* my girlfriend." He gripped his knife tighter, sounding irritated that she'd even suggested it.

"Then why's she so 'territorial'?"

"Our families have known each other since before we were born," he said. "She's like a sister to me."

"A sister who's looking at us like she wants to claw our eyes out," Alyssa muttered.

Jamie looked skeptical. She clearly didn't believe him.

And while I wanted to believe him, I didn't either. Just like I didn't believe he was being honest with me Monday at lunch.

There was something *off* about him. And as attractive and magnetic as he was, I didn't trust him.

"Anyway," he continued, returning his focus to me. "Why would you think I'm drunk?"

"Because you're acting like you did on Saturday, when you said you were drunk," I said simply.

"And what way is that?" He tilted his head, curious.

I paused to think about my answer.

"Like you're not a total jerk," I finally said.

He chuckled at my response. "I promise I'm only a 'total jerk' half of the time," he said, and while I thought he meant it as a joke, all it did was back up my feeling of needing to be on guard around him.

There was something about him that felt cold, inhuman, and *dangerous.*

Maybe it was the same way humans had always felt around me. An instinct that made them keep their distance.

"So, you came over here because you're in the good half of your moods today?" I asked, unable to keep the sarcasm from my tone.

"I came over here because I wanted to have lunch with you." He raised his fork to his lips and took a slow bite of his burger patty for emphasis.

Somehow, he managed to make the act of eating look temptingly dangerous.

I sighed, since this conversation was going nowhere. "Did your memories from Saturday night start to come back or something?" I asked, figuring I might as well get to the point.

The point being that he hadn't been drunk that night. If he'd just admit it, then maybe I could forgive him for the way he'd treated me on Monday.

He froze, and his eyes looked pained. "They didn't," he said, his voice hard as stone.

I held my gaze with his, hoping he could tell that I didn't believe him.

He continued eating, and once it was clear that he wasn't going to elaborate, I glanced down at my watch.

Since Zane had gotten to the dining hall late, lunch was almost over.

Thank God. I needed to get out of this situation, ASAP.

"We should head to class," I said to Alyssa and Jamie, standing up before they could answer.

"Wait." Zane wrapped his hand around my wrist as I reached for my tray, and my heart stopped.

His lack of body heat shocked me just like it had the first time he'd touched me. It was like he wasn't human. Which he technically wasn't, since we were all witches. But last time I'd checked, I still had a normal body temperature, as did Alyssa when we'd held hands during the spell last night.

"What?" I asked, and it came out ruder than I'd anticipated.

"Come to dinner with me tomorrow night. In DC. There's a restaurant there I think you'll like."

I blinked, shocked. "Why do you want to go to dinner with me?" I asked, my guard up more than ever, especially after the Courtney incident.

"Because I want to get to know you better." He watched me under his long, hypnotizing lashes, waiting for an answer.

I stared at him like he'd lost his mind. Which, from this entire experience at lunch, he might have.

"It sounds suspiciously like you're asking me on a date," I finally said.

He looked at me in challenge, and my heart leaped like the traitor it was around him. "That's exactly what I'm doing," he said.

"Why?" I asked again, and then I clarified, "I thought you 'weren't the relationship type.'"

"It's dinner—not a marriage proposal," he said. "So, are you free tomorrow night?"

I stepped back and pulled my wrist out of his grip, surprised by how easily he let go.

"I'll think about it," I said, since I was far too jumbled to decide on the spot.

And because even though I knew I should say no, a part of me clawed at my heart to say yes.

"If you decide you want to join me for dinner, find me tomorrow and let me know," he said coolly. "But no matter what you choose, I want you to make me a promise."

"What promise?"

"I want you to stay with either Alyssa or Jamie at all times. To be safe."

Alyssa and Jamie looked as clueless as I felt about why Zane would ask this of me.

This was also the quietest the two of them had ever been. It was like Zane had cast some sort of intimidation spell over them.

"Is this about Drake?" I asked Zane, since judging by his reaction at the party, it was the only thing that came to my mind. Although I couldn't imagine why he would care, given that he apparently didn't remember anything from that night.

"There's been some talk," he said. "Drake and his friends want to 'get you back' for what happened at the party."

"You're the one who threw him into the wall," I said. "Shouldn't they want to get *you* back?"

"I wouldn't have had to throw him into the wall if you hadn't been turning down his advances. He blames you—not me."

Jamie scoffed. "Guys are such dicks," she said.

Zane's icy eyes sharpened. "Not all of us."

"Only half the time." I rolled my eyes, somehow earning an amused smirk from him.

Alyssa shuffled back and forth on her feet, holding her tray. "We *really* have to get going," she said, and I noticed that the other students were starting to filter out of the dining hall as well.

I refocused on Zane, who was leaning casually back in his chair, as if getting to afternoon classes was the least of his concerns. He looked dark and dangerous, like he was daring me to give him an answer. Everything other than him turned into a muffled blur.

Say yes, the thought flittered through my mind, as if

being close to him was hypnotizing me into submitting to his request.

"I'll see you around," I said instead, and then I spun on my heel and hurried out of the dining hall, freeing myself from the tether between us.

CHAPTER TWENTY-FIVE

After classes were over for the day, Alyssa followed me into my room.

"What was that about today with Zane?" she asked what I knew she'd been dying to say since we left lunch.

"I'm as clueless are you are." I dropped my backpack onto the chair at my desk. "His mood swings are as crazy as Edward Cullen's."

"Except he eats like the wolves." She giggled, and then she imitated me in a high-pitched voice. "'You like meat.'"

"Oh my God." I covered my face with my hand. "That was super awkward, wasn't it?"

"Yep," she said. "Although it could have been worse?"

I lowered my arm back to my side. "This isn't helping."

"Sorry." She shrugged. "Want a drink?"

"Yes," I said. "I *definitely* want a drink."

She grinned. "Any preferences?"

"Wine. I trust you to pick a good one."

"On it." She hurried to her room, and I used the time while she was getting the drinks to change into comfy sweatpants and a *Hunger Games* t-shirt.

Alyssa returned with an open bottle of red wine in one hand and two clear plastic glasses in the other. She'd also changed into comfy clothes, and we sat on the rug where we did the spell last night.

She glanced at my shirt. "Trying to channel your inner Katniss in case we have archery practice again tomorrow?" she asked as she poured our drinks.

"You're starting to understand how my mind works," I said with a smile.

I never thought I'd feel this comfortable with anyone except for Lara, but Elementals Academy was throwing all types of surprises at me.

She handed me my cup, we tapped our glasses together, and each took a sip. Even though I knew next to nothing about wine, I could tell this was a good one.

"So…" she started, her eyes wide with curiosity. "Are you gonna go on that date with Zane tomorrow night?"

"I don't know," I said, then I thought about it further. "I guess I want to go on a date with the person he showed me he was on Saturday night. Not the person he showed me he was on Monday."

"What about the person he showed you he was *today?*"

"That's what I'm confused about," I said. "It's like there are three versions of Zane, and I don't know which is the real one."

"All three of them are real. But I'm gonna bet on the one you saw Saturday night." She smiled and held up her cup of wine. "He said he was drunk, and they don't call it truth juice for nothing."

I sipped my wine, since I didn't feel the need to repeat for the millionth time that I didn't think he was actually drunk that night.

Alyssa's eyes lit up. "I have an idea," she said.

"Another spell?" I smiled at the thought, since it had felt empowering to tap into the Universe and take things into my own hands.

"Not a spell," she said, and I sat back, disappointed. "Wait here."

She returned with a small, purple wooden box carved with swirly decorations and hands holding a crystal ball. She took off the top of the box, removed a deck of purple cards from inside it, and started shuffling them.

"Are those tarot cards?" I asked.

She stopped mid-shuffle. "How did you know that?"

"My mom has a pack that she keeps in the living

room. She never uses them, but I played with them sometimes as a kid."

Alyssa's eyes narrowed. "Are you sure she's not a witch?"

"I'm sure," I said. "She would have told me if she was."

"But you were adopted," she said. "Magic is genetic. She had no reason to think you're a witch, too. Maybe that kept her from telling you."

"Maybe," I said. "But wouldn't the Elders who talked with her last week have noticed if she was a witch?"

"Hm," she said, thinking about it. "You're right— they would have been able to tell if your mom's a witch. Maybe she's just one of those humans who has a tiny trace of magic in their blood. They're the ones who tend to be most interested in tarot and stuff. It would explain why she was drawn to you and adopted you."

"Makes sense," I said, since Kate had said something similar about Lara. "Anyway, I'm guessing you want to do some sort of love reading about me and Zane?"

"Not a love reading," she said. "I want to do a general reading about *you*. If the cards feel like telling us something about Zane during the reading, they will."

"I'll trust your expertise," I said, even though after what had happened at lunch, Zane was front and center in my mind right now.

I didn't want him to be, but he was. And I couldn't push him out, no matter how hard I tried.

"Tarot's fun and interesting, but I'm not the best at it," Alyssa continued as she returned to shuffling the deck. "Spells are more my thing. Other than elemental magic, of course. But I felt drawn to do a reading for you, so I'll try my best."

"Cool," I said, and then she gave the deck one final shuffle and handed it to me.

"Pick seven cards," she said.

"Any specific way I should pick them?"

"Whatever way feels right."

I fanned them out on the floor between us, picked seven cards, then handed them to her.

"Are you happy with the order of the cards?" she asked.

"Yes." I didn't need to think twice about my answer.

"Okay." She gathered the rest of the cards, put them to the side, then flipped over the cards I'd drawn. Two cards at the top, one below it, three below that one, and then one at the bottom. She nodded as she flipped over each one.

I leaned forward, curious. "What do they mean?"

"I'm seeing strong earth energy from two powerful people in your past," she started, pointing to the top two cards—the King and Queen of Pentacles. They featured a strong, stoic-looking man and woman respectively, with crystals emerging out of the ground around them. "This could represent your birth parents."

"But you said they have earth energy," I said. "Not air."

"They do," she said. "Which is interesting."

Interesting.

Another way of saying, *I don't know how to reply right now, so I'm gonna say something to fill the silence and make things less awkward.*

Next, she moved on to the card below it. The High Priestess. The woman depicted on it—with long black hair and pale skin—looked like me.

"This card is your present," she said. "The High Priestess represents intuition and magic. I feel like it means you're tapping into the magic inside you."

"Makes sense," I said.

"Next is where things get really interesting." She pointed to the three cards below it.

The Knight of Cups: A prince in shining armor on a white horse.

The Two of Cups: A couple bathing in a pond in the moonlight.

The Seven of Swords: A man holding a sword, looking warily over his shoulder while crows flew through the sky.

"I don't like the look of that third card," I said with a nervous chuckle.

"It's nothing to worry about," Alyssa said quickly. *Too* quickly for me to fully believe her. "But it's something to think about. Because I'm close to positive that this has to do with Zane. And I think it's warning you to watch your back for any deception he might throw your way."

I instantly grew more alert. "So the cards are saying that Zane is lying about something."

"It's a possibility."

"Got it," I said, since it was something I'd already thought myself, anyway.

Then I looked to the card at the bottom. The Tower. A stone turret being struck by lightning, half of it crumbling into a stormy ocean. "That one looks pretty ominous, too," I said.

"The Tower isn't *always* bad," she said in a way that made me think it tended to be bad. "In this position, it's saying that a monumental change is coming your way— and that this change is going to happen quickly and powerfully."

"Hopefully it means I'll quickly get full control of my magic," I muttered.

"It likely has to do with your birth parents, and you coming into your magic," she said. "The big mysteries here are why your birth parents have such strong earth energy around them, and what's going on with Zane. Because according to the cards, there's a true connection between the two of you. But it feels like something might be hidden in that relationship, and that it'll cause upheaval in your future."

"But we can always change our future, right?" I asked. "It's not set in stone?"

"The cards serve as a guiding force to help you make decisions about your future," she said. "But this change I'm seeing *will* come. The question is how you—and possibly Zane—are going to handle it."

"You're talking about me and Zane like we're a couple." I shook my head slightly, since after this past week, I didn't see that happening anytime soon.

"There seems to be a real love connection there." She shrugged and motioned to the card of the couple bathing in a lake under the moonlight. "At least that's what the cards are saying."

"Interesting," I said, since I couldn't deny the connection I'd felt with him Saturday night.

While he was drunk. Or not drunk. Whatever.

The deception Alyssa was talking about made a huge amount of sense. Because how was I supposed to be able to trust someone who wasn't being honest with me?

I couldn't. I needed to be wary, like the guy on the Seven of Swords card.

"Seems like the cards are warning me to stay away from him," I concluded.

"The decision is yours," she said. "Trust your gut."

At that, my stomach growled. Loudly.

"I think my gut is telling me it's time for dinner."

"Dining hall or common room?" she asked.

"Common room." I didn't have to think twice, since if I went to the dining hall, I might see Zane—and I didn't want to talk to him until I figured out how I wanted to move forward.

CHAPTER TWENTY-SIX

The library at Elementals Academy was the tallest building on campus, and it was what I imagined the Alexandrian Library had looked like before it had burned down. The dome in the center of the ceiling was supposed to let in the sunlight, although since it was the middle of winter and the sun was setting at an ungodly early hour, there was no sunlight right now. The floors were a brilliant white marble, with gold columns going all the way up to the ceiling, so it felt like a palace.

The first level of the library was full of scrolls, and the books became more modern on each level, up to the newest ones on the fifth floor.

I'd made myself comfortable at a desk in the back of the third floor to study for the History of Magic quiz coming up on Tuesday. It was a simple quiz for most of the students, but I had a lot to catch up on.

However, I'd barely created my first few flashcards.

Because my traitorous mind kept wandering to Zane.

I'd come to the library for lunch to avoid seeing him, and to avoid deciding about the date tonight. I had no idea if it was because I was worried I'd give in and say yes, or if I hated the thought of rejecting him in person. Now I was here because I didn't want to go back to the dorm and be questioned by Alyssa.

It was rude of me. And cowardly. I was ashamed of myself for not being a braver, more confident person.

It was just that I didn't know what to do. It was like my heart and my mind were at war with each other, and I had no prior experiences on which to base my decision.

I contemplated it for a few seconds, then realized I was staring blankly at the wall again instead of focusing on studying.

I was stuck in thought-loop limbo.

At this pace, there was no way I'd be ready for the quiz on Tuesday.

Maybe I just needed to go on the date and see what happened. Then I could stop all this wondering. No date could be worse than this all-consuming limbo.

I pulled out my phone to text him, then remembered —we'd never exchanged numbers.

Seemed like the only way I'd be able to reach him would be by finding him in person.

So I gathered my stuff, left the library, and headed

toward the water dorm. There'd been an unseasonably warm spell this morning, so I hadn't bundled up like I had a few days ago.

I stopped once I reached the entrance of the dorm, since my watch wouldn't open the front door, and waited. It wasn't long before one of the students—a tall, model-esque girl who I assumed was a descendent of Aphrodite—came out. She was so involved in something on her phone that she held the door open for me without thinking twice about it.

I entered the foyer, which was empty, since there was another thirty minutes before dinner.

Please be here, I thought as I walked down the hall toward Zane's room.

I stopped in front of his door and heard muffled voices inside. Relief crashed through me, and I raised my arm to knock.

It must not have been fully closed, because it swung open on the second rap... revealing Zane and Vera sitting on the bed, his arms wrapped around her in an intense, loving embrace.

It was *not* the way you hugged someone who was "like a sister" to you.

My heart dropped into my stomach.

He'd lied. Of *course* he'd lied. I should have known as much, given the way Vera had glared at him during lunch.

I was *such* an idiot.

I should have trusted my brain and not my heart.

I was standing there shell-shocked when Zane looked up and his gaze met mine. His eyes flashed with surprise, and then guilt as he pulled away from Vera.

Vera glanced at me over her shoulder and smirked in victory.

"Summer." Zane's voice was strained, and he pushed Vera out of his arms to stand up. "This isn't what—"

I reached for the handle of the door and slammed it shut before he could finish his sentence. Angry heat rushed through me, starting in my core and flowing out to my fingers and toes. It *consumed* me.

Suddenly, the metal door handle *burned,* as if I'd touched a hot stovetop.

I gasped, pulled my hand off it, and examined my palm.

It wasn't red. And it didn't hurt anymore.

Curious, I brushed the pad of my index finger over the handle.

It was normal temperature.

I must have been so angry that I'd imagined it.

I had no idea how that was possible, but I'd think about it later. Because I felt like the biggest idiot on the planet. And right now, I needed to get out of this dorm, and as far away from Zane and Vera as possible.

CHAPTER TWENTY-SEVEN

I returned to my room, threw my backpack on my bed, then knocked on Alyssa's door.

When she opened it, she was in jeans and a silk purple top, her hair perfectly curled. One of her eyes had shadow on the lid, and the other didn't. Jamie was sitting on the floor in front of the full-length mirror, also in the middle of getting ready to go out.

Confusion flashed in Alyssa's eyes. "I thought you were gonna be at the library late tonight?" she asked.

"Change of plans." I walked over to sit on her bed, then filled her and Jamie in on what had just happened, from the beginning until coming back here.

"I *knew* he and Vera were together," Jamie said once I was done. "I have a sixth sense for these things."

"I feel like an idiot for believing him," I said.

"You couldn't have known," Alyssa said. "For what it's worth, I believed him, too."

"But isn't it weird that Vera didn't say anything at lunch?" I asked. "If they were truly together, wouldn't she have come with him to our table?"

"Maybe they aren't officially together?" Alyssa suggested. "And since you turned him down, she decided it was time to make her move?"

"I didn't turn him down," I pointed out.

"You avoided the dining hall today," Jamie said. "And you didn't try to talk to him until last minute. It's basically the same as turning him down."

"Yeah," I said, since I knew it was true. "But I don't understand his motive. Why ask me out if he has a thing with Vera? Why lie about it?"

"He's a descendent of Aphrodite," Jamie said. "They get off on playing with people's hearts."

"I thought that was descendants of Zeus." I chuckled, even though I wasn't at a point where I could make light of the situation.

"We don't do it on purpose." She frowned. "I genuinely like all the guys I date. But the descendants of Aphrodite toy with people for fun. They're cruel about it."

"We don't even know if he's a descendent of Aphrodite," I reminded her. "He hasn't been claimed."

"He has the most classically good looks of any guy in

the school," Jamie said. "He's clearly a descendent of Aphrodite."

"It doesn't matter who he's descended from," I said. "All that matters is that he's a lying asshole."

They both nodded in agreement.

"What about the thing that happened when I left?" I asked, ready for a change of subject. "When my hand burned."

I studied it again, checking for any blisters, but there were none.

"Easy," Alyssa said. "Well, not so easy to do, but easy to know how it happened."

"How?"

"Super powerful air elementals can control the temperature around them," she said. "They can cool it down or heat it up. You must have been so angry that you did it by accident."

"More like humiliated," I said. "But I guess it's similar enough."

"Both are strong emotions," she said. "And you tap into your magic the most when your emotions are triggered."

"True," I said, glad that at least one thing about tonight made sense.

My thoughts immediately returned to the intimate way Zane had caressed Vera, and my heart jumped into my throat again.

"You're still upset," Jamie observed.

"I'm upset at myself," I said. "Zane's an asshole. He's shown that to me multiple times. So why do I care so much? Why am I hoping he'll knock on my door, try to apologize, and say that what I saw was a big misunderstanding?"

From the way Alyssa bit her lip, I could tell she knew as much as I did that Zane wasn't going to chase after me with any apologies.

If he'd wanted to do that, he would have run after me when I was hurrying out of the water dorm.

"There's always something alluring about the bad guys," Jamie finally said. "I've been there myself. And I've found that the best remedy is to find someone else to distract you."

"I already told you that doesn't work for me," I said, frustrated.

"Well, Alyssa and I are getting ready to hang out in the fire dorm," she continued. "You should come. It'll be good to at least have a fun night out with your friends."

I frowned at the thought of the fire dorm, since that was where Drake lived. He'd been avoiding me since Zane threw him into the wall, but I didn't want to risk running into him if I didn't have to.

"Why don't we go into the city instead?" Alyssa jumped in. "There's a wine bar there that I *love.*"

Jamie shifted uneasily. "Shane's expecting me at the

fire dorm," she said. "But the two of you should definitely go to the city. That wine bar is fun."

"I'm sure it is," I said, even though I had a feeling that their definition of a fun night out on the town was probably very different from mine. "But I don't have a fake ID."

"You're a witch," Alyssa said. "You don't need a fake ID."

"What do you mean?"

Her eyes twinkled with mischief. "Remember how humans tend to be wary of us?"

"Of course," I said, since I'd only dealt with it for my entire life.

"It stops them from questioning us," she said. "Or carding us. Plus, the owner of this place is a witch. He knows my family. And a bunch of regular, non-elemental witches go there, too. We'll be fine." She paused and eyed me, as if trying to figure out my reaction. "So, what do you say? Are you in?"

I took a second to think about it, and found I was relieved at the thought of going off-campus for the night. Maybe I'd feel more normal, and not like a late-blooming elemental witch who had basically no control over when I used my magic. Plus, I wouldn't have to be looking over my shoulder to make sure Zane and Vera weren't around. Drake, too, given that Zane had warned me about him yesterday at lunch.

Although given Zane's track record, he was probably lying.

And there I was, thinking about Zane again.

Maybe Alyssa was right, and a night out would get him out of my head.

"I'm in," I said before I could change my mind.

"Good choice." She walked over to her fridge and opened it. "You know what's also a good choice? Pre-gaming."

"Yes. It. Is." Jamie emphasized each word.

Alyssa popped open a bottle of champagne, and I joined them in getting ready, determined to get Zane off my mind and have some fun. I was *not* going to let an asshole like him get me down.

And after how the night had started with finding Vera in his room, it could only get better from here.

CHAPTER TWENTY-EIGHT

The Uber ride from the academy to downtown DC was about a half hour long. We drove through a street packed with college students waiting in lines to get into the clubs and bars, but continued on to a quieter part of the city.

Finally, the driver stopped in front of a row of rundown brick buildings. A Thai restaurant, a minimart with a fading neon sign with half of the bulbs burnt out, and a hardware store.

"You sure this is the right place?" the driver asked.

I gave Alyssa a wary look, since I was wondering the same.

"This is it!" she chirped, and then she hopped out of the Uber.

I shrugged at the driver and got out of the car, wrapping my coat tighter around myself. No other cars drove down the street, and the only other person there was a tall man on the sidewalk across from us. The distinct scent of curry floated out of the Thai restaurant, and the minimart appeared empty.

Unease crept down my spine.

"Are you trying to get us shot?" I whispered to Alyssa, since there were plenty of dangerous neighborhoods in DC. "Or kidnapped?"

"No one's getting shot or kidnapped." She rolled her eyes. "Come on. It's this way."

She reached for my hand and pulled me toward the narrow alley between the Thai place and the minimart. Spiderwebs draped between the tops of the buildings, and I thought I saw a furry rodent skitter next to one of the walls.

"We're *not* going in there," I said.

"You're my new best friend. I wouldn't bring you somewhere that would get you killed," she said. "Just trust me."

"I trust you. But I have my limits." I motioned to the alley and scrunched my nose in disgust. "Explain."

"Fine. Ruin the fun." She pouted. "Have you ever heard of a speakeasy?"

"The hidden bars that served alcohol a century ago, when drinking was illegal," I said, since of course I knew what a speakeasy was.

"Yep." She smiled, as if I'd passed some kind of test. "And we're going to one."

"That way?" I glanced in the alley again and looked up to search for spiders.

I couldn't see any right now, but there was no way they weren't there.

"It wouldn't be hidden if it was out in the open," she said. "I promise you'll like it. But if you hate it, we'll leave. Deal?"

"Fine," I gave in. "Although you really should have brought a weapon to defend us against the spiders. And the rats."

"We're witches," she said simply. "The spiders and rats are afraid of *us*."

"Then I guess the fear will go both ways."

I was on guard as we walked down the alley, and if there were any spiders or rats, none of them came near us.

I was just letting my guard down when something scurried behind us.

I yelped and spun around… and the back of my hand whammed into the brick wall behind me.

"Ow." I cradled my hand and examined the damage. It was scraped, with a bit of blood in the center.

"You okay?" Alyssa asked.

"Just a scrape," I said. "I thought you said there weren't any rats?"

"I said the rats won't mess with us. Not that there weren't any of them."

With that, I hurried to the exit of the alley. Alyssa stayed by my side.

The area behind the buildings was wide enough for a single car to drive through, although there were no cars, because it led to a dead end. It smelled like garbage, thanks to the dumpsters behind each building. Soda cans and other various bits of trash littered the ground.

We approached a deteriorating wooden door with no sign above it. The only marking was a small bunch of grapes that looked like they'd been drawn in black permanent marker.

Alyssa reached for the handle, and the door creaked open.

A wooden staircase the same width as the door led down to a basement. An antique chandelier lit the stairwell, and red and gold wallpaper lined the walls. It looked like we'd stepped into a well-kept historic house.

"Told you it would be nice," Alyssa said, and she started to head down. "Make sure to close the door behind you. We have to keep this place a secret. Especially from the rats."

I closed the door as tightly behind me as possible and looked skeptically down the stairs.

"Don't worry," she said. "It's rat free. I promise."

"All right." I followed her down, keeping my eyes

out for rats the entire time. As promised, there were none.

There was another door at the bottom—this one super ornate. She knocked, and a slot opened at about eye-level.

"Password?" a gruff, male voice asked from the other side.

"In vino veritas," Alyssa said, and then the slot closed, and the door opened.

The guy on the other side looked just like the big bouncer I'd imagined he'd be.

"Welcome," he said, and then he handed us each a gold token—the kind they had at old-school arcades. It had the same bunch of grapes engraved on it that had been drawn on the alley door. "The first drink is on the house."

He glanced at the bar in the back, which had a cash register that looked like it had come straight out of the 1800s. The entire place—with its cabaret tables, red velvet sofas, and low lighting—looked over a century old. If not for the people in modern clothes, I would have thought we'd traveled back in time. And while it was busy, it wasn't so busy that it would be impossible to grab a table.

A man in his forties or fifties stood behind the bar. He waved at Alyssa, and she waved back.

"Come on," Alyssa said. "Let's get our first round."

We walked to the back, where the bartender—who I assumed was the family friend who was a witch—was waiting.

"Alyssa," he greeted her warmly. "How's your family been?"

"Wouldn't know," she said with a casual shrug. "Haven't talked to them since getting back to school."

"I'm sure they don't want to distract you from your studies," he said, and then his friendly eyes went to me. There were wrinkles around them—he was definitely on the older side of my original guess. "Are you the air elemental who just started at the academy?"

"I didn't realize people were talking about me outside of the school," I said.

"The DC coven's favorite topic of conversation is the academy." He leaned forward, looked around to check if anyone was listening, and lowered his voice. "I think most of them are just jealous that you youngsters get elemental magic and we missed out."

"Maybe my parents need to be talking with you all more often," Alyssa mumbled. Then she looked over at me and smiled, her expression totally changed. "Summer, this is Alistair. Alistair, this is Summer. As you guessed, she's the new air elemental. And my new suitemate."

"Welcome to DC," he said, and he glanced at my token. "What'll it be?"

"Um…" I checked out the rows of wine bottles on the shelf behind him. "I guess a chardonnay."

"You're not a descendent of Dionysus, are you?" he asked.

"Definitely not," Alyssa spoke for me. "Give her the Meursault chardonnay. I'll take the Cakebread cabernet."

"Coming right up." He grabbed the bottles, uncorked them, then poured us our glasses. "The bottles are yours. I'll keep them here until you need refills."

"Perfect." Alyssa slid him her token, and I did the same.

"I'll send a cheese platter over as well. Witch's discount." He winked and handed us our glasses.

"Thanks," Alyssa said, and then she found us a round table against the wall, and we sat down and started to drink.

"I feel bad taking all this stuff for free when our academy credit cards can easily pay for it," I said after the waitress dropped off our cheese platter. "I don't know much about fancy cheese, but these look expensive. I bet those bottles of wine are expensive, too."

"Don't worry about it." She brushed it off the way only people who grew up with money could do. "Try the brie. It should go great with your wine."

Of course she was right—the light-colored cheese she'd pointed to was delicious.

"What did you mean when you said your parents

should be talking with the DC coven more?" I eventually asked her.

"Oh. That." She frowned. "My parents don't like that I have elemental magic."

I put my wine glass down, confused. "I thought elemental witches were the most powerful witches?"

"They are," she said. "But my family's witch history goes way back. My parents are super intense about tradition and studying the ancient ways."

"Like spells and tarot cards," I said.

"Exactly. They're skeptical about elemental magic. They think it's dangerous, or unnatural, or something. I don't get it. They weren't happy when I got my magic, and they definitely weren't happy when I started at Elementals Academy. But they won't go against Kate and the Elders, so here I am."

"It bothers you," I said. "That's why you never talk about them."

"They're disappointed in me for something I can't control. And I like my elemental magic. So I'm never going to come to an agreement with them about it." She reached for her wine and took a long sip.

"That's tough," I said, and I took an equally long sip of my wine.

"Yeah," she agreed, and she pasted her usual bright smile on her face. "Anyway, what do you think of the place? It's cool, right?"

"Very," I said. "Thanks for getting me off campus. I needed this."

"Anytime. That's what friends are for."

From there, we chatted for hours. Alyssa was *really* good at making random chitchat, which was great, since that had never been a strength of mine. She wasn't a big reader, but we liked a lot of the same TV shows, so it was easy to fall into long discussions about those.

Before we knew it, I'd finished one bottle of wine, and Alyssa had finished two. Everyone but Alistair and the wait staff had left the bar, and the lights went up.

I glanced at my watch—it was 2:30 AM.

"Witching hour," Alyssa said mischievously.

"That's a thing?"

"Nah." She finished the last drops of her wine. "I made it up." She giggled, clearly feeling the wine.

I joined in, since I wasn't immune to the alcohol, either.

Not like Zane, I thought, and then I chided myself for thinking about him on what was supposed to be a Zane-free night out. I'd done such a good job so far tonight. But I supposed talking with Alyssa about our mutual love of *The Vampire Diaries* could do that to a person.

Although it was going to take a bit of time to get over the fact that she was on Team Stefan and not Team Damon.

"Last call!" Alistair shouted—obviously to us, since

we were the only ones in the bar. "Do you need me to call you an Uber?"

"I've got it," Alyssa replied, bringing out her phone. "But thanks for the offer."

"Anytime," he said. "Get home safe."

"We have the power of the elements on our side," Alyssa said as we stood up and headed toward the door. "We're the *definition* of safe."

With that, the bouncer opened the door for us, and we headed back up to the alley.

CHAPTER TWENTY-NINE

Alyssa stumbled up the steps, and I linked my arm with hers to make sure she didn't fall.

"Your alcohol tolerance is better than mine," she said, and then she hiccupped.

"I had half as much as you," I reminded her. "And my tolerance is terrible. We've just been drinking for *hours*, so it isn't hitting me as hard since the drinks are spread out."

"Right." She rolled her eyes. "You're no fun."

"One of us needs to make sure we don't get eaten by rats." We reached the top stair, and I opened the door.

"I already told you," she said. "Rats are the ones who are scared of us. We're natural rodent repellers. And insect repellers. They can smell the magic in our blood."

"I guess that explains why mosquitoes have never

liked me." I glanced around the back alley, searching for rats.

It was still littered with trash, and it stunk of garbage. Maybe some people liked the super secretiveness of the speakeasy, but this was definitely a one-and-done activity for me.

Just when I thought the coast was clear, something moved in the dumpster we'd have to walk by to get out of there. I glanced over my shoulder to see if there was another way out, even though I knew from earlier that it was a dead end.

"Come on." I tugged on Alyssa's arm to get her to walk faster, then held my breath, as if that could keep the dumpster rodent away.

"This could be good target practice," she said. "Use your magic to kill a rat."

"I'm not *killing a rat*," I hissed. "Well, not unless—"

I didn't have time to finish my sentence, because a person turned the corner around the alley to stand in our path. A broad-shouldered man who had to be over seven feet tall. He wore no shirt, was more muscular than a body builder... and he was carrying a thick, wooden club with spikes protruding out of the end.

I instinctively took a few steps backward.

"Get out of here," Alyssa told him, sounding confident even though she must have been half his size.

He opened his mouth and growled.

The air around him shimmered and blurred.

I squinted to try to focus. Maybe I'd drank more than I'd thought?

But then the space cleared up, revealing a big, hairy monster with hunched shoulders and a tiny head completely out of proportion with his body. His wide nose was so hooked that it covered the center of his top lip, and two pointed teeth curved out from his lower jaw.

Not again.

I cursed and did a quick sweep of the area, ready for someone to come to our rescue. Nicole and Blake were supposed to keep the DC area clear of monsters.

Why weren't they here?

The monster raised his club above his head, locked his gaze on us, and roared.

Alyssa shrieked and hurried backward, but she tripped over one of the soda cans and fell on her butt.

I ran back as quickly as I could without falling myself and reached down to get her.

I wasn't quick enough.

The monster wasn't fast, but it had huge legs, so the few steps it took were enough to block our way to both the speakeasy door *and* the alley's exit.

Crap.

He opened his mouth into what might have been a smile, walking slower now that we were cornered. He was definitely enjoying this.

"What do you want?" I screamed, praying he could understand.

He roared again and swung the club through the air.

"I take it that means you don't want to be friends," I muttered, and then I held out my hands, gathered my magic, and tried to *push* a gust of wind out of my palms.

Nothing.

The monster made a low sound that might have been a laugh and took another step toward us.

I glanced at Alyssa, who was still frozen on the ground. "Get off your butt and *help me!*" I said.

She blinked, and like a switch had flipped, she jumped back onto her feet. She wobbled slightly, but stayed standing. Then she pointed her palms out, and two soda cans blew across the alley.

One of them soared over the monster's head. He struck the other with his club like it was a baseball and sent it flying straight at me.

I held my hand out to protect myself and squeezed my eyes shut, bracing for impact.

Nothing hit.

I opened my eyes. The can was frozen mid-air, Matrix style. I felt a connection to it, like I had with the stones during the spell. So I sent it back his way, like I had when Courtney had flung the crystals at me.

It missed him and hit the wall instead. But there were more than enough soda cans on the ground...

Alyssa threw a gust of wind at the monster, along with two more cans.

One smacked him in the forehead.

He growled and charged, club high and ready to bash my head in.

I flinched back and spun on my heel. But one of the club's spikes slashed through the material of my jacket and down my arm, from below my shoulder nearly to my elbow. It stung, but I barely felt any pain. Probably thanks to adrenaline.

The monster raised the club to strike again, but a gust of wind pushed him back a few steps.

Alyssa.

She'd saved us a few seconds at most. Which meant it was now or never.

Instinct took over.

I put out feelers with my mind and tuned into the soda cans littering the ground. It was like there were invisible tentacles coming out of my hands, connecting with the cans. There must have been twenty or thirty of them in all.

I raised the cans off the ground and shot them at the monster.

They pelted him one after another, forcing him back like bullets hitting a bulletproof vest, until he was standing next to the dumpster.

The dumpster hummed with energy. It drew the

feelers in my mind toward it like a magnet, and their invisible tentacles wrapped around the entire thing.

It was mine to control now.

Power buzzed through me. Using all the force I could muster, I screamed and used my mind to roll the dumpster sideways as fast as it could go, plowing at the monster and pinning him to the wall. His ribcage audibly crunched. I pushed the dumpster more, not stopping until the monster's eyes widened so much that they were about to pop out of his head.

Energy drained out of me, and my head dizzied with exertion.

Unable to hold onto the dumpster anymore, I let it go.

The monster let out a long, defeated breath. The club fell out of his hand, his eyes closed, and his head drooped over the rim of the dumpster like a rag doll.

All I could hear were my heavy, exhausted breaths.

Alyssa stepped tentatively to my side. "Did you kill it?" she asked, her voice shaking.

My mind flashed back to my encounter with the harpy. "No," I said. "He would have disappeared if I did."

"Right." She brought her palm to her forehead. "Duh. The wine's getting to my head."

"I noticed." I glared at her, since if she'd been less drunk, maybe she would have been more helpful.

She sucked in a sharp breath inward, looking at me like I'd slapped her.

Icy wind blew past my cheeks.

She blinked a few times, and her glassy eyes became more focused. "We can't let him hurt anyone else," she said, and then she marched toward the monster—only stumbling once—and picked up the club. It was half her height, and she looked ridiculously small holding it. But she took a few steps back, stared at the club with determination, and threw it like a javelin at the monster's head.

Wind guided the club's way, and the top of it slammed into his head, crushing his skull.

The monster flickered a few times, then disintegrated into ash, his pants and club the only things left behind.

"There." She wiped her hands off on her jeans and smiled. "*Now* it's dead. Although it shouldn't have—"

Before she could continue, the throbbing in my right arm intensified. I reached for it and groaned. My jacket was slashed where the spike had torn through it, its edges wet with blood.

Alyssa cursed and ran over to inspect it.

"It's bleeding, but I don't think it hit an artery," she said. "How badly does it hurt?"

"I'll survive," I said through clenched teeth, and I glanced at the space between the dumpster and the wall where the monster had been. "What the hell was that?"

She pressed her lips together, silent for a second. "I have no idea," she finally said. "But whatever it was, it shouldn't have been here."

I glanced at the door to the speakeasy. "Should we go down there and warn them?"

"Monsters don't hunt regular witches," she said. "They'll be fine. That thing was after us—not them."

"Great. That's just great." I looked around the alley, paranoid. "Do you think there are any more of them?"

"I don't know." She checked her watch. "But our Uber's still waiting for us. So let's not stay and find out."

CHAPTER THIRTY

The Uber driver looked hesitantly back at me when we got into the car. Specifically, at the bloody slash on my arm.

"You all right there?" he asked.

"I'm fine," I said. "We were drinking a lot. I tripped."

"It looks pretty bad…"

"I'm *fine*," I said, irritated now. "Can you hurry up and get us out of here?"

His eyes widened—maybe he'd realized that something dangerous was lurking around, or maybe he was intimidated by my witchy aura—and he started driving.

"Are you sure you don't want me to drive you to the hospital?" he asked when we were a few blocks away.

"We want you to drive us to Emerson-Abbot Academy," Alyssa said the official name of Elementals Academy. "We have a doctor there who will check her out."

"As you wish." He sighed and kept driving.

Alyssa turned to me. "I don't have Nicole's number," she said. "You should text her to let her know you need her help." She glanced at the slash on my arm, her message clear.

I needed Nicole to heal it for me.

I reached for my phone and winced from the rush of pain.

Alyssa reached for my phone. "Give it to me."

"I can do it." I opened my text chain with Nicole. The last message was her telling me not to worry about what had happened in archery the other day.

It had only been three days ago, but it felt like forever.

My thumbs hovered over the keys as I thought about what to say.

Got attacked by a monster in DC. Am with Alyssa. We killed it, and we're fine, but it slashed my arm a bit, and I could use help.

I pressed send, and her reply came nearly instantly.

Where are you?

In an Uber coming back to school, I replied. *Be there in twenty.*

Come straight to Kinsley Cottage. Don't talk to anyone on your way here.

I responded with a thumbs-up, then handed the phone to Alyssa so she could read the texts.

"I've never been inside Kinsley Cottage," she said, giving me back my phone.

"Well, it sounds like that's about to change."

Kinsley Cottage was a Victorian-style house with a wraparound porch. It looked nothing like the Grecian buildings on campus—it could have been plucked out of Salem.

Alyssa and I hurried toward it, and I was glad that the dark of night hid the gash along my arm. Not like I had much to worry about, since the only people walking around campus this time of night were drunk stragglers.

Nicole was waiting at the front door when Alyssa and I walked onto the porch, and she hurried us inside a cozy living room that also had a Northeast feel to it.

Blake was pacing around inside, and Kate stood from where she was sitting on the couch.

"You reek of alcohol," Kate said the moment we walked in. "Let me get you some water." She hurried out of the room to what I assumed was the kitchen.

Nicole walked to me and examined my right arm. "It's just a surface wound," she said. "Should only take a few seconds. Can you take off your jacket?"

Kate returned with two cups of ice water. She handed

the first one to Alyssa, who gratefully took it and plopped into the closest plush armchair.

"I'll hold your water until Nicole heals you," Kate told me.

I removed my jacket, trying extra hard not to let it brush too much against the slash on my arm. The wound was only a few inches long, but it stung like crazy.

Nicole placed her hand on it and closed her eyes.

I waited for a burst of warmth, or for the skin to feel like it was sewing itself up, or something of the sort.

Nothing happened.

Nicole opened her eyes and stared at the slash. "Hm," she said, like a doctor trying to diagnose mysterious symptoms.

"What?"

"Let me try again."

She closed her eyes, but again, nothing happened.

After a few quiet seconds, she drew her hand back. My blood was on her palm, and confusion was splattered across her face.

"Are you okay?" I asked.

"I think so," she said slowly, and then she looked to Alyssa. "Use your fingernail to scratch yourself."

"How deep?" she asked. "Like the one Summer has on her palm?"

Nicole's eyes went straight back to me. "What did you do to your palm?"

"I tripped into a wall and scratched it on the brick." I shrugged, not wanting to admit that I'd also shrieked at the sound of a rat.

Although after the monster attack in the back alley, I didn't feel as stupid about being so on guard.

"Let me see," Nicole said.

I raised my left palm so she could look. There were a few dots of dried blood, but nothing serious.

Nicole laid her palm on top of mine, closed her eyes, and my hand tingled with warmth.

When she opened her eyes and removed her hand, the scratch was gone.

"The problem isn't me," she said. "It's you. More specifically, the wound on your arm."

"You really can't heal it?"

"It appears not." She chewed at her lower lip, troubled. "But it looks like it could use a few stitches. The campus doctor can take care of it."

"Why do you have a campus doctor when you can heal people?" I asked.

"I can heal physical injuries," she said. "Regular sicknesses or diseases are out of my realm."

"So witches can get sick?"

"Usually not the demigods," she said. "But the others do."

"Oh," I said. "Interesting."

She studied me and narrowed her eyes, like she was trying to figure me out. "Do you get sick?"

"Not really." I shrugged.

"Ever?"

"Not that I can remember." I took a moment to think back, but came up with nothing. "After getting here, I assumed it was because of the whole witch thing."

"Interesting," she said in a way that I could tell meant that this was *not* a normal witch thing.

Of course it wasn't.

Being abnormal was what I excelled at around here.

"I'll call the doctor and tell her to get over here with whatever she needs for a few stitches," Kate broke into the conversation. "Then I need you to tell us everything that happened tonight in the city."

CHAPTER THIRTY-ONE

The doctor looked at Nicole suspiciously when Nicole asked her to fix up my wound.

"Why not use your magic to heal her?" she asked.

"It's complicated," Nicole said in a tone that made it clear she wasn't open to answering any questions. "But everything is under control."

I didn't believe her. I didn't think the doctor did, either.

When she numbed my arm and stitched it up, I averted my eyes the entire time. Luckily, whatever she'd used to numb it was super effective, although from the amount of Advil she recommended I take each day, I knew it was going to hurt later.

It was going to need some bandaging and cleaning for the next few days, but it was nothing Alyssa couldn't help me out with.

"Tell no one of this incident," Kate told the doctor after she was finished. "Understood?"

"Yes," the doctor said, although from the way she glanced at Nicole again, it was clear that she was worried.

"Thank you," Kate said. "You can go now."

The doctor packed up her stuff, and Kate saw her out.

"You're going to have to wear long sleeve shirts until we've figured out a solution to this," Kate said to me after she returned. "If people see your injury, they'll ask questions."

"There's going to be a scar," I reminded her. "I won't be able to hide it forever."

"We'll get to the bottom of this before that's an issue." She sat down in one of the armchairs, looking ready to get down to business. "Now, I'm going to need the two of you to tell us what happened tonight, starting from the beginning. Why were you in DC?"

"Just wanted some time away from campus," I said before Alyssa could say anything about Zane.

My guy problems had nothing to do with this, and I really wasn't in the mood to share it now.

Or ever.

She continued to pepper us with questions, although of course we didn't get to the confrontation with the monster until the end.

"Something strange happened when I killed it," Alyssa said. "It turned to ash."

Blake's brow knitted in confusion. "Are you sure?"

"Yes," she said. "I'm sure."

He looked to me, and I nodded in confirmation.

"Interesting," he said, and Kate looked equally as surprised.

Nicole was quick to jump in. "The two of you did a good job. I'm glad your training was put to use," she said, and then she focused on me. "Although the way you describe using your magic is certainly interesting."

"Let me guess." I sighed. "No one uses their magic like that?"

"Not that we know of," Kate said. "But like I told you last week, there's a first for everything, and there are always exceptions to the rules. Take Nicole, for instance. She's the only elemental witch able to heal others. Her magic is different, but that doesn't mean it's bad."

"And you're cool with not knowing why your magic is different?" I asked Nicole.

"It is what it is." She shrugged. "I roll with it. Plus, being the same as everyone else is boring."

"I guess so," I said. "I just wish I had answers."

"These things can't be rushed," Kate said. "We'll figure something out. We just need to be patient."

"Sure," I said, since she had no way to know that.

Alyssa bounced her legs impatiently. She was clearly bursting with a question, but didn't want to interrupt.

"So, what type of monster was it?" she asked once we reached a break in the conversation. "And I thought there weren't supposed to be any monsters in DC?"

She looked to Nicole and Blake when she said that last part.

"There aren't," Nicole said. "We take care of them before they can enter the general area." She glanced at my arm, as if the monster and her inability to heal my injury might be related. "I don't know how we missed this one."

"But what *was* it?" I repeated Alyssa's first question.

"I'm going to have to research it further," Kate said. "Do either of you think you can sketch what it looked like?"

"I can try," I said. "But fair warning—the worst grade I ever got in high school was in my painting class."

"I'll give it a go," Alyssa said casually—the way people talked when they knew they were good at something but didn't want to brag about it.

"Sounds like that's the best move," I said, and Alyssa smiled at me, as if telling me she had it covered.

But I was surprised that Kate even needed a sketch. I thought she'd have an immediate answer to what we were dealing with.

Maybe she did, but she didn't want to tell us? Because she didn't want to cause any alarm?

From the concerned look in her eyes, I didn't think that was the case. She looked truly baffled.

"I appreciate your help," she said. "I hope you know that you're safe inside the school, thanks to its protective barrier."

"Weren't we supposed to be safe in DC, too?" I asked.

"You should have been," Blake grumbled.

Nicole took his hand, and he leaned slightly toward her. "It's not your fault," she reassured him. "We couldn't kill a monster when we didn't know it was there."

"That's the problem," he said. "We *should* have known it was there."

The three of them were quiet, and I knew they agreed with him.

"We'll get it sorted out," Kate said, which I was beginning to think was her response to anything she didn't have an answer to. "But I think it'll be best for all students to stay on campus until then. I'll speak to the Elders tonight and make an announcement in the morning."

"What are you going to tell them?" I asked, since I hardly imagined that "two freshmen fought an unknown monster and barely escaped with their lives" was going to keep everyone calm.

"I'll figure something out," she said. "In the meantime, I'd appreciate if the two of you kept what happened tonight to yourselves."

"Sure thing," I said, since I was finally starting to not be the main topic of conversation around campus, and I had zero desire to change that.

"Alyssa?" Kate asked.

"Sure," she said. "But my friends know we went to DC tonight. They'll probably ask what happened."

"Lie," Blake said simply.

Alyssa went rigid. "Right," she said. "Will do."

He nodded approvingly.

"Thanks," Kate said. "And don't worry. We've faced a lot, and have always gotten through. I'm sure we'll have answers soon." She paused to look out the window, then refocused on us. "But it's late, and I'm sure you're tired and want to get some sleep."

I wasn't tired, but I knew a dismissal when I heard one.

Kate wanted us gone so she could discuss this further with Blake and Nicole.

And from the way they were acting, I had a feeling that whatever was happening, it was far more of a problem than they wanted to let on.

CHAPTER THIRTY-TWO

A lyssa passed out quickly after we got back to our suite.

I rushed to my laptop and opened a fresh tab on my browser. The internet would have so much information that it would be impossible to know what was true—the only place that had reliable information was the New Alexandrian Library—but at least it was a start.

Unsure where else to begin, I clicked on the images button and did a generic search for *Greek mythology monsters*.

None of the monsters pictured looked like what we'd faced in the alley.

So I went to Wikipedia and found a list of Greek mythological creatures. There were over a hundred of them listed, and I clicked *every one* of them, reading the articles to find something that somewhat matched. It felt like it took forever.

None of them were close.

So I returned to Google and searched for more Greek mythological creatures.

Still nothing.

Eventually, I got so frustrated that I typed *mythological monster big ugly nose* into the search bar. It was silly, but what did I have to lose?

The first image that popped up was of a troll.

It was the closest thing to what we'd seen in the alley... and a few of the photos showed trolls holding wooden clubs.

Relief filled me. Because finally, I felt like I was getting somewhere.

I searched the word *troll,* and there were a bunch of pictures of the kids' toys with tall, bright-colored hair and gems for belly buttons. Definitely not what I was looking for. So I extended it to *troll mythology...* and bingo.

Lots of pictures of trolls, and some of them nearly exactly resembling the one in the alley. I read the articles, and everything made sense except one major detail.

Trolls weren't part of Greek mythology.

They were from *Norse* mythology.

That couldn't be right.

My History of Magic textbook only mentioned Greek

mythology. If mythologies other than Greek existed in the real world, surely someone would have mentioned it at some point?

I thought back to everything that had happened since Nicole and Blake had knocked on my door, searching for any places I might have heard or seen something about Norse mythology.

That was when it hit me.

The variety of textbooks about mythology that Zane had on his bookshelf. Including Norse. He'd chalked it up to having "broad interests," and then he'd told me I should go to sleep. As if he didn't want to discuss it any further.

Did he know something?

Probably.

Did I want to talk to him?

Absolutely not.

Besides, the only books that were considered reliable sources of information were those found in the New Alexandrian Library. There was no way to know where he'd gotten his.

But now that I had a starting point, the library was exactly where I needed to go.

At some point while I'd been thinking, the birds had started to chirp. I looked out my window and saw that the sky was tinted pink. Sunrise.

A quick glance at my watch showed that it was 7:30 AM.

I'd been so focused that I hadn't noticed myself getting tired. Now, exhaustion hit me like a tsunami. My eyelids felt heavy, my head was foggy, and my body felt weak.

As much as I wanted to push through, there was no way I'd get anything productive done like this, especially if I was reading a book instead of staring at the bright computer screen.

So I changed into my pajamas, got ready for bed, and fell asleep the instant my head hit the pillow.

I woke up feeling totally refreshed. When I picked up my phone, I saw that I'd slept until noon.

Right under the time was an emergency notification from Kate that said in all caps: ALL STUDENTS, READ IMMEDIATELY.

I swiped on it and was brought to an announcement on the school's app.

Students of Elementals Academy,

. . .

Due to an unforeseen circumstance, all students are prohibited from leaving campus for the next week. Barriers have been placed around campus to ensure compliance to this temporary measure. This is for your own safety.

More information to come, but for now, do not panic. The Elders, teachers, and I have everything under control.

Your headmistress,
  Kate

Jamie had sent me multiple texts.

There were no messages from Alyssa, which I assumed meant she was still sleeping.

One of Jamie's texts asked if something had happened in the city last night.

Nothing at all, I wrote back with the shrug emoji. *Gonna be at the library all day. Let me know if you hear anything!*

Her only reply was a thumbs-up. I figured she was at lunch gossiping about what was going on. The dining hall was likely a madhouse.

One that I had zero intention of walking into.

After a quick shower, I re-dressed my wound. It was

gross to do it myself, but it was already starting to heal. Then I made myself a peanut butter and jelly sandwich, ate it as fast as humanly possible, gathered my stuff, and headed to the library.

I didn't get very far.

Because when I walked by the common room, I saw that *he* was there.

Zane.

He was sitting alone on the couch, facing the front doors.

And he was staring right at me, his icy eyes sharp and focused, like a predator waiting patiently for its prey.

CHAPTER THIRTY-THREE

Zane tilted his head—like he was beckoning me to join him—and I froze.

Should I ignore him and continue to the library? It would be cold, but I didn't owe him my time. Or, if I didn't want to be a total bitch about it, I could just tell him I was on my way to the library to get work done, and that I didn't have time to chat.

Then again, he did have a Norse mythology book in his room. Maybe he knew something that could help me?

There was also no denying that if he wanted to say something to me after what had happened last night, I was curious about what it would be. And if I didn't hear him out, I'd be wondering what he'd wanted to say to me instead of staying focused on my research.

So I tightened my grip on the strap of my backpack

and marched over to the couch, although I didn't sit down.

He looked relieved at my decision. "Hey," he said casually. "I was hoping you'd be here."

"Why?"

"Because I wanted to talk to you about what happened last night." He moved to make room for me on the couch, as stoic as ever.

I shifted uncomfortably on my feet and glanced at the empty space next to him. "Sure," I said, although instead of sitting next to him, I sat on the opposite end of the couch.

If he was disappointed, he didn't show it.

I leveled my gaze with his, waiting for him to speak.

"Like I told you before, Vera's an old family friend," he started. "When you walked into my room, I was comforting her."

"The two of you looked pretty close," I said, remembering the intimate way they'd embraced. It was the way you embraced someone you loved.

Although that was really all I'd seen—them sharing a hug. It wasn't like I'd walked in on them naked in bed together.

Even if I had, Zane wasn't my boyfriend.

He'd asked me out on one date, and I never got back to him. He could do whatever he wanted with Vera, even though on some deep level, the thought of his being with her felt fundamentally wrong.

"We *are* close," he said. "She's like a sister to me. And she's been through a lot these past few years."

"It's fine," I said, although given the way Vera had looked at me when I'd walked in—like she was happy I'd seen them like that—I wasn't sure she felt the same. "You don't have to explain."

"I want to."

I sized him up, and could tell he was dead serious. "Okay," I said, since if he wanted to open up to me, I wasn't going to stop him.

"Before Vera and I got our magic, she had a boyfriend," he started. "They'd been together for years. But there was an accident a few weeks earlier. A car accident. Her boyfriend didn't make it."

"Oh. Wow." I frowned and lowered my gaze, caught completely off-guard. "I'm so sorry to hear that."

"Vera doesn't want anyone here to know," he continued. "She doesn't want people to pity her."

"So why are you telling me?"

"Because I know how what you walked in on must have looked to you," he said. "I wanted you to know the truth."

"Okay." As I processed what he'd told me, I caught myself playing with my fingers, so I dropped them onto my lap. "I understand."

"I hoped you would," he said. "But that wasn't the main reason I wanted to talk to you." He watched me carefully, waiting. The space between us on the couch buzzed with the energy passing between us.

"What's the main reason?" I finally asked, totally clueless about what he was getting at.

"You melted the deadbolt on my door."

"What?" I sat straighter, caught completely off-guard.

"You heard me."

"I have no idea what you're talking about," I said, although I had a flashback to how hot my hand had felt after I'd slammed his door shut.

So much had happened since then that I must have pushed it to the back of my mind.

"The deadbolt was melted in place so much that we couldn't get out," he said. "Blake had to come over and use his fire magic to fix it. He joked and said that I must have really pissed off a fire elemental, and I went along with it to cover for you. Vera did, too. Probably because she wants to hold it over my head."

"I thought she was your best friend?"

"She's like a sister to me," he said. "It's different."

"Oh," I said, although since I'd never had any siblings, I didn't know what that was like. "And I don't know what I did to your door. It wasn't on purpose."

"But you did it." He glanced around, as if making sure no one was coming. Then he scooted closer, his gaze locked on mine. "You're not actually an air elemental, are you?"

My heart stopped in my chest.

I wasn't sure if it was because I felt like he'd caught me doing something wrong—even though not knowing what type of magic I had wasn't wrong—or because there was only about a foot of space between us.

Probably both.

It was like he was trying to seduce the answer out of me. Which clearly wouldn't work, since I had no answer.

I looked away from him, taking a few moments to organize my thoughts before meeting his gaze again.

"I failed the placement test, and I don't use wind when I use my magic to move things," I said, laying out the facts. "Now I apparently melted the deadbolt on your door so much that you couldn't force it open with your super strength. I have no idea what I did. But you're the expert in mythology. If there's something else you think I am, please tell me. Because I'm dying to figure it out myself."

The air chilled between us so much that it felt harder to breathe. I shivered, although I resisted rubbing my hands over my arms, because I didn't want him to think that whatever he was doing was fazing me.

"You really don't know," he finally said, and the air warmed again.

"No." I sat back in relief. "Do you?"

"I don't."

"Bummer. Because it would be great if someone around here had an answer." I smiled slightly, surprised by how comfortable I felt in his presence given everything that had happened between us.

He moved closer, so his hand was only inches away from my leg. We both glanced down at it, but he didn't move.

I didn't move away, either.

"There's another reason I wanted to see you today," he said.

My breaths quickened from the intense way he was staring at me—like he was trying to see into my soul. His eyes were so mesmerizing that it should be illegal.

"What's that?" I spoke slowly and carefully.

"Why did you come to my room last night?"

My head buzzed, my heart felt like it slowed down, and I felt more vulnerable than ever.

I also saw no reason not to be honest with him.

"I never gave you an answer about that date," I finally said.

"So you came by to tell me yourself." His breaths were slower, too—maybe he was as affected by me as I was by him.

Or maybe he was just trying to drag answers out of me.

"I didn't have your number." I shrugged, trying to be

casual about it. "I didn't know what else to do. I tried to knock, but your door was already open. I didn't mean to walk in on anything."

"I'm pretty sure I dead-bolted it." He tilted his head, like I was a curiosity he was trying to figure out. "But it doesn't matter. Because you came over to give me your answer. So—what was it?"

I swallowed to get ahold of myself.

But before I could reply, his watch buzzed.

He glanced at it and frowned.

"What's wrong?" I asked.

"It's Vera." He sounded annoyed. "She needs my help with something."

"Is everything okay?"

"She's fine, but I do have to go," he said. "What are you doing tomorrow for lunch?"

My tongue felt like it twisted in my mouth, and I wasn't sure I could properly make words. "I don't know," I said, relieved that I sounded relatively human. "Why?"

"Because I want to take you out."

My heart leaped. But there was a big thing he was forgetting…

"We can't leave campus," I reminded him.

"I know," he said. "There's a place on campus I have in mind. I'll pick you up and we'll walk there together. Tomorrow at 11:30?"

This conversation felt like it was happening so quickly that I couldn't keep up enough to think about my answer. But given the fact that he'd come here specifically to apologize, and that my gut was telling me to trust him, I knew exactly what I wanted.

"Okay." I finally said. "Sure. That sounds great."

"Cool." He smiled. "Give me your phone."

"Why?"

"I think it's about time we exchanged numbers. It'll be a lot easier than hunting each other down around campus every time we want to talk."

"Right." I felt like an idiot for not realizing that immediately—and for apparently only being able to speak in single-syllable words. Then, realizing that he was waiting for me, I dug inside my bag for my phone. "Here," I said, handing it to him.

His fingers brushed mine as he took it, and an icy-hot wave of exhilaration rolled through my body.

He entered his number, typed something out, then his watch buzzed with a text.

I eyed it warily.

Was Vera messaging him *again*?

"I texted myself so I can have your number, too," he said, and then he handed me back my phone and started to stand up. "See you tomorrow."

"Wait," I said, and he stilled, looking taken aback— like he thought I was about to change my mind.

"What's up?"

"You had all those books on mythology in your room," I said quickly, not wanting to hold him up. "What do you know about Norse mythology?"

"A bit," he said warily. "Why?"

"Because I want to learn about it. For one of my classes."

I felt bad about lying, but I'd promised Kate I wouldn't say anything about the monster.

His brow creased. "I don't remember learning about Norse mythology my freshman year."

"It's a special project," I said, since that *wasn't* a lie. "That's where I was heading right now—to the library, to do some research."

"Got it." He glanced at the door, like he was getting antsy, then looked back to me. "Like I said, I don't know much. But if I were you, I'd look through the scrolls. They're hard to search through, but there's a lot of good information there."

"Thanks," I said. "I'll do that."

"Good luck," he said, and his expression turned serious. "I hope you find what you're looking for."

"Me, too," I said. "And I hope everything's okay with Vera."

"She'll be fine," he said. "And it's not supposed to be too cold tomorrow, but since I know you're used to Florida weather, make sure to dress warmly."

"We're doing something outside?" I glanced out the window in horror.

"Not saying any more. It's supposed to be a surprise." He backed toward the exit, looking as mischievous as ever. "See you tomorrow, Summer."

Then he was out the door before I could reply.

CHAPTER THIRTY-FOUR

Groups of students huddled around the study tables in the library, chatting amongst themselves. I didn't know them, since most of them were earth elementals, so no one paid me much attention as I walked to the back where the scrolls were on the ground floor.

As I'd learned on my tour the first day, the ancient scrolls were magically protected, so it wouldn't hurt them to be handled. And *all* the books in the library were enspelled so a person could read them in their native language.

The aisles looked the way I'd always imagined the shelves of the original Great Library of Alexandria would look—a bit dusty, with scrolls of various sizes and shades of cream piled on top of each other in cubical cubbies. This section of the library even smelled old, like

I'd stepped into a museum. The shelves were tall enough that there were occasional rolling ladders to get to the topmost ones.

And there were *so many* scrolls.

Immediately overwhelmed, I went to the librarian for help. She was kicked back in an office chair behind a desk, her nose stuck in a romance novel, oblivious to anything going on around her.

I rested my elbows on the desk and leaned forward to get her attention.

"Hi," I said after she looked up. "How do you recommend I navigate the scrolls?"

Confusion crossed her face, as if I'd spoken to her in Greek. "Why would you want to do that?" she asked.

"Research." I used the same excuse I'd used with Zane.

"Most anything you need to research for class can be found on floors three and above." She glanced up at the top floors, which all looked down to below. "The rest is just here because it needs somewhere to be archived."

"Thanks," I said. "But I really just want to know how to sort through the scrolls."

She took a deep breath, as if she were hesitant to tell me. "They're alphabetical," she finally said. "Starting from the left and going to the right."

"Organized by subject?"

"Basically." She shrugged. "But fair warning—'organized' isn't a word I'd use to describe the scrolls. It takes a lot of digging to find what you want. People can get lost in there for days."

"Sounds tiring."

"Like I said, there's good stuff in the upper floors," she said. "And it's much easier to navigate the shelves up there."

If it hadn't been for my chat with Zane, I would have taken her up on it.

But something about the way he'd told me to look through the scrolls made me feel like he knew what he was talking about.

"I'll try my luck with the scrolls first," I said. "Thanks."

"Have fun," she said, as if she expected it to be anything but, and then she went right back to reading her novel.

I walked back to the shelves of scrolls and headed slightly right of the middle of them, since that was where the N section would be. Hopefully there would be a section devoted to Norse mythology.

There were no letters to label any of the shelves, so I supposed I would have to dive in and figure it out from there.

Lowering myself to my knees, I reached for a medium-sized scroll in the bottom-most box in front of me. Whatever paper the scrolls were made of—maybe papyrus—felt positively ancient. I didn't want to damage it. But reminding myself that it was spelled so it wouldn't disintegrate from my touch, I unrolled it and read the title at the top that was scripted in beautiful calligraphy: *Persephone and the Pomegranate.*

P was too far down the alphabet. But I still sang the alphabet song in my mind to double check.

After confirming that P was, in fact, after N, I put the scroll back. Then I rotated around, faced the shelves to the left, and chose the thinnest scroll in the cubby.

It was something about an Ouroboros. Below the title was a detailed drawing of a snake eating its tail.

Out of curiosity, I reached for another scroll in the same cubby.

Perseus and Medusa.

After checking a few more scrolls in the same cubby, I learned that it was a mix of O's and P's, with an occasional Q shoved in there for good measure. There didn't seem to be any rhyme or reason for it, but I was glad it at least stayed within the same section of the alphabet.

It took *hours* before I started to find an occasional scroll that mentioned Norse mythology, although no trolls were mentioned in them. I'd also tried the T section to search for a scroll about trolls, but came up with nothing.

By the time I returned to where I'd left off in the N

section, the sun had long set, and only a few straggling students remained in the library.

Apparently, even the earth elementals had better things to do than study on a Saturday night.

Then my phone buzzed with a text. Alyssa.

Where have you been all day? she asked.

The library, I replied. *Trying to figure out more about that monster from the alley. Want to come help?*

It took her a few minutes to reply.

I drew that sketch for Kate. She'll take it over from here.

Cool, I replied, since I wasn't surprised Alyssa didn't want to spend hours in the library. Then I added, *This is taking forever. It's looking like I'll be here all night.*

Good luck!

I put my phone away and got back to it.

Eventually, I found something in one of the top shelves.

The Norse World Tree.

I carried it down the ladder with me, situated myself on the floor, unrolled the scroll, and started to read.

Below the title was an intricate drawing of the Tree of Life—what the Nordics called the World Tree. There were various worlds—or realms—within and around the tree. One of them was the World of Giants and Trolls, which was represented in the drawing by a huge glacier.

Trolls.

Finally, I was onto something.

But the scroll only talked about the basics of each realm. It had no information about the gods or creatures that lived within them.

However, there still was some information in the scroll that I could go on. Because the World of Giants and Trolls was called Jotumheim.

So I rolled up the scroll and put it back into the section where I'd found it, even though it had become clear that other people who explored the scrolls had just shoved them back into random cubbies in the general area.

Next, I headed to the area where it seemed like the J section would be. After a good amount of time rummaging around, I managed to find the center of it.

It was nearly 5 AM before I finally found a scroll about Jotumheim—the ice realm of the World Tree.

First it talked about the jotunn, who were also called giants. Despite their name, they were human-sized, and were basically immortal frost people. They were also supposed to be extremely beautiful. The descriptions of them reminded me of the vampires in *Twilight*, if the *Twilight* vampires had frost magic.

I unfurled the scroll as I read, disappointed that pretty much all the information in it was about the giants.

Finally, way at the bottom, it mentioned trolls.

The trolls were said to be monsters of the wilderness

of Jotumheim. The description of them was on point with what I'd seen of the monster in the alley—down to the fact that they liked using wooden weapons.

But the information about them in the scroll ended there.

I gazed back up at the looming shelves, exhausted by the idea of rummaging through more scrolls to find anything else about Jotumheim.

I glanced at my watch—6 AM. Sunday morning.

I had enough time to get four hours of sleep, then clean myself up for my date with Zane. He clearly knew something about Norse mythology, so maybe he'd tell me something helpful during our time together.

It was as good of a reason as any to abandon my search in the scrolls for now.

And while I had no idea why Zane had pointed me this way, I did know that tomorrow, I was going to find out.

CHAPTER THIRTY-FIVE

Somehow, I woke up feeling refreshed and ready for my date with Zane.

Well, maybe not *ready*. I was definitely nervous. But it was going to be fine.

At least, that was what I kept telling myself.

After finishing getting ready, I checked the weather, glad that Virginia was still having its "heat wave." Still, I dressed in what was probably too many layers. One big thing I'd learned since coming up north was that it was better to have too many layers than not enough.

I double-checked my reflection and got that strange feeling again—like I was being watched.

Maybe the dorms were haunted. But they weren't old enough to have ghosts, since they'd all been built after the school was founded a few years ago. Unless ghosts liked to haunt new buildings, too.

Ghosts weren't something we'd touched on yet in my classes. And I really hoped they were one of the things in mythology that were fiction and not reality. They'd always given me the creeps—whenever a movie trailer came on that had ghosts, I had to cover my eyes.

Before I could contemplate it further, there was a knock on the bathroom door.

"Come in," I said, and Alyssa opened it and peeked inside my room.

"Where are you going?" she asked.

"Long story," I said. "But basically, I ran into Zane yesterday. He explained some stuff about what was going on with Vera, and he asked me out again. So... we're going to lunch. Right now."

I was surprised by how cool and collected I sounded about it.

Probably because with so much else going on, I didn't have the emotional bandwidth to get as excited/nervous/anxious as I might have been otherwise.

"You're dressed like you're about to venture out in the Arctic," she said.

"He's taking me someplace outside," I told her. "I figured I should dress warm."

"Did he tell you where he's taking you?"

"He said it's a surprise."

"Hm." Her brow creased with worry. "Text me when

you get there to let me know where you are? Just in case."

She didn't have to explain any more, since after what had happened Friday night with the troll, I understood why she was on edge.

"Sure," I said, and then my watch buzzed with a text.

Zane, letting me know he was outside the front door.

"He's here," I told her. "Gotta run."

"Good luck!" she said. "And remember to text me."

"Will do." I took a deep breath, did a final mirror check, and hurried out.

Zane was waiting outside the air dorm, wearing dark jeans and a long-sleeve black t-shirt. No jacket required, thanks to his ice magic. He was also carrying a hiking backpack filled to the max.

What did he have in store for us?

He gave me a small smile, his eyes twinkling with amusement. "I see you took it to heart when I said to dress for the outdoors," he said.

"We can't all be water elementals who aren't affected by crazy-cold temperatures," I teased him back.

Despite everything, I was surprised about how natural it felt to be around him. It was like we were back to how things had been between us the night of the party.

It felt *right.*

"Air elementals can change the temperature around them, too," he said, but then we both quieted, since after our chat yesterday, we both knew there was more going on with me than being a simple air elemental.

It was yet another concern I'd blocked out while busying myself with researching the scrolls.

"Anyway," I said, taking the few steps down to join him. "Where are we heading?"

"How do you feel about nature?" he asked.

"I like it," I said, since I'd always loved sitting out amongst the trees in the patio behind my house. "I mean, I haven't had much time to explore much beyond the beach and the swamps, but I'm open to it."

"Swamps?" he asked, amused again.

Apparently, I was funnier than I realized. If so, maybe I *was* a descendant of Hermes, like the others had mentioned during that first lunch.

"The Everglades in Florida," I explained. "Flat, grassy, and teeming with alligators. But it's not as bad as it sounds."

"I'll take your word on that," he said, and then he led the way to wherever we were heading. On our walk there, he asked me how it was going in my classes, and he listened intently as I told him about my mishaps in the elemental magic sessions.

He wasn't a major talker, but I liked that. I could tell that he was truly listening as I answered his numerous questions.

Or maybe he was trying to make sure I didn't have time to ask him questions of my own. After our conversation in his room after the party, I wouldn't put that out of the realm of possibility.

We passed the earth dorm, and he continued until we reached the start of the woods. There were a few trails leading into the trees, which were bare of leaves, looking cold and uninviting.

I stopped and checked them out skeptically. "We're not supposed to leave campus," I said.

"We *can't* leave campus," he replied. "There's a boundary spell stopping us from leaving. But a good chunk of the woods is still part of campus. The earth elementals come here a lot to practice their magic."

"Got it," I said. "But I thought we were going to lunch?"

The peanut butter sandwich I'd scarfed down after getting back from the library early this morning wasn't going to hold me over for much longer.

"We are," he said. "What do you think I have in my bag?"

"We're having a picnic?" I asked.

"Yep. I figured it would be more private than going to the dining hall," he said. "Plus, this is one of my favorite places on campus."

"I thought water elementals loved the lake."

"And *I* think we shouldn't be put into boxes based off our element or godly ancestor," he said. "Come on. Let's see what you think."

I paused to think about it. Because maybe I shouldn't be going into the woods with a guy I'd only known for a week.

But for reasons I couldn't fully explain, I trusted Zane. I didn't feel like he would lead me to harm. I was safe with him.

I'd also promised Alyssa that I'd let her know where we were going.

So I took my phone out of my bag and quickly texted her that Zane and I were going on a picnic in the woods.

"All good?" he asked after I put the phone away.

"Yeah," I said. "It was just Alyssa."

"Cool," he said. "Now, are you ready to adventure? I promise there won't be any alligators."

I smiled, since now I was the one who was amused. "Lead the way."

I managed to make it through the trail without *too* many mishaps with branches. The walk took us to a circular clearing surrounded by trees and rocks, and even though there were no leaves on the trees, I imagined it would have looked like a winter wonderland if there was snow.

Zane opened his pack, brought out a warm-looking, blue plaid blanket, and laid it out on the ground.

"Sit," he told me, and I did as he asked. The blanket was thick enough that I didn't feel any of the small rocks on the ground.

My stomach growled—I was glad we were eating soon.

He apparently heard it, because he glanced at me and smirked in amusement. Then he kneeled and reached into the bag, bringing out little plastic baggies full of different cheeses and meats. I watched, impressed, as he arranged a charcuterie board on a small wooden slab.

Once it was set up, he handed me a bottle of Coke.

"Thanks," I said, opening it and taking a sip.

"I saw you drinking it at lunch," he said. "Figured you'd like it. There's water, too."

"This is perfect," I said with a smile.

"I also brought sandwiches for when we're done with the cheese," he said. "And dessert."

"Wow," I said. "Impressive."

"I try."

"You succeeded."

We shared a smile, then started on the charcuterie board. I went straight for the cheese, but Zane only ate the meat.

"Is meat the only thing you eat?" I asked.

"It's my preference."

"But you can't *only* eat meat," I said. "You need other vitamins and stuff."

"I've never had any issues." He shrugged, and as I thought about how to possibly respond, he broke into a smile. "I'm kidding," he said. "Of course I eat other foods."

As if to prove it, he picked up a piece of cheese and ate it. It didn't look like he enjoyed it, but he swallowed it down anyway.

"Satisfied?" he asked.

"Very."

I picked up a piece of cheese and chewed on it, completely aware of the fact that he was watching my every movement.

"So," I started. "About those scrolls."

"How'd it go?"

"Slowly," I said. "I was there all night."

He nodded, like he hadn't expected anything less. "When you want good information, you have to dig for it."

"I barely got any information," I said, and then I relayed what had happened in the library.

"It sounds like you *did* find something," he said once I was finished.

"Not much."

He scooted closer, so his knees nearly brushed mine.

My skin tingled where it was close to his.

"Why the interest in Norse mythology, anyway?" he asked, his breath cool and minty even though we were eating meat and cheese.

"I told you," I said, although I was so focused on the connection between us that I could barely pay attention to what I was saying. "I'm doing research for a class."

"And instead of trying to research why you can somehow use both air and fire magic, you chose trolls?"

"I don't think I can use fire magic." I held my hand out palm up, like Blake had done in my apartment, and tried to create fire. "See? Nothing."

"What you did to my door wasn't nothing."

"Did you bring me out here to launch an inquisition?" I asked, suddenly defensive.

"No," he said. "I brought you out here to do this."

The next thing I knew, he leaned forward and pressed his lips to mine.

My heart leaped, and a wave of energy rushed through me and traveled through every nerve in my body, like I'd been struck by lightning. It *burned*. But not hot. It was cold, like my blood was turning to ice in my veins.

I felt like a mosquito that had flown into a trap and been zapped.

I gasped, leaned back, and pressed my fingers to my lips. The pain subsided, but my body still buzzed with energy.

Zane looked as shocked as I felt, and his ice-blue eyes were *glowing*, the colors swirling like hurricanes in his irises.

He ran the pads of his fingers over his lips in amazement. "Impossible," he said slowly.

"What did you do to me?" I backed away, trying to resist the urge to reach for his hands. Because even though he'd somehow attacked me with his lips, I felt more drawn to him than ever. "What's going on with your eyes? What *are* you?"

"Your soulmate," he said, sounding as shocked by it as I felt.

My heart felt like it fell into my stomach. "Is this another joke?"

"No joke." He pulled his phone out of his pocket and held it up with the front-facing camera toward me, so I could see my face on the screen like a mirror.

My eyes were glowing and swirling too, although they'd stayed green, just like his had stayed blue.

The buzz in my body stopped, and my eyes returned to normal, too.

I looked up at him in question. "Soulmates don't

exist," I said. "If they did, Alyssa or Jamie would have mentioned it by now."

"They don't exist for Alyssa or Jamie, or for anyone else at this school," he said, still studying me in wonder. "But they do for me. It's why I couldn't stand it when that half-blood bastard of Ares wouldn't take his hands off you at that party."

"I thought you were too drunk to remember that night?"

"I lied," he said. "I remember everything."

Betrayal—and confusion—surged through me. "If what you're saying is true, and we're soulmates," I said, the word feeling ridiculous on my tongue. "Then why did you lie to me?"

"Because I was just as confused as you are," he said, and from the way he stared at the ground and shook his head, I believed him. Then he raised his eyes back up to meet mine and continued, "But it's starting to make sense now. It's why I felt so compelled to bring you here. To keep you safe."

"To keep me safe from *what?*"

He wasn't making any sense.

Unless he knew about the troll?

Before he could reply, something rustled in the forest behind me.

I turned around and saw a person making their way through the trees. A woman with pale skin and strawberry-blonde hair, wearing white jeans and a matching tank top.

She had to be freezing.

And she looked too old to be a student, so she had to be a teacher.

Alyssa must have told someone we were out here, and a teacher came to bring us back to the main part of campus. Which was the worst timing ever, given the crazy-bomb Zane had just dropped on me.

The woman stepped into the clearing and smirked. "Look at you, sleeping with the enemy," she said to Zane, and then she reached for something in her back pocket. "So, who's going to be the one to kill her? You, or me?"

CHAPTER THIRTY-SIX

The air around us chilled.

"Neither," Zane said, and then he held his hands up and shot two long icicles toward her.

She jumped, flipped over them, and the ice crashed into the trees behind her. When she landed, she was holding a dagger—that must have been what was in her back pocket—and she stood in fighting stance.

"Gone soft, have we?" she said to Zane.

"She's my soulmate," he said, his voice stern and steady. "She stays alive."

"No can do." She shook her head and smirked again. "One of ours was killed Friday night—a troll. Your girlfriend's blood was all over the alley where it happened. I used it to trace her here."

Panic seized my lungs, and I glanced over my shoulder at the forest behind me.

I should run. Get as far out of the woods as possible, go to Kate, and tell her the school had been breached.

But what about Zane? I knew he could hold his own, but I didn't want to leave him here with *whatever* that woman was.

"Well, that explains the sudden interest in trolls," Zane muttered.

I looked back and forth between them, confused. "Who are you?" I asked her, and then I turned to Zane. "And what do you have to do with all of this?"

The woman snickered and swung her long hair over her shoulder. "You haven't told your *soulmate* what you're doing at this school?" she asked Zane.

He shot more icicles at her, and she danced around them.

But the side of her arm was now pink. One of them must have hit her.

I needed to protect myself.

What could I use as a weapon?

The answer came to me quickly—the cutlery we'd used for the picnic. More specifically, the knife to slice the blocks of cheese.

I opened my hand behind me so my palm was facing the food, thought about the knife, and *connected* with it with my mind like I had with the dumpster. Even though I wasn't touching it, I could feel the shape of it, and it hummed with energy, ready to obey my commands.

I got a firm hold of it and sent it flying at her shoulder.

She screamed, yanked it out, and threw it on the ground. Blood stained the strap of her white tank top.

Somehow, she'd kept her hand wrapped around her dagger the entire time.

The corner of her lip quirked up in amusement. "You missed."

"I didn't."

I'd originally been aiming for her heart, but then I'd changed my mind. Because she knew something. I could feel it. And if she was dead, I might never find out what that something was.

I called the knife back toward me, and it floated in front of my hand, its sharp tip facing the woman.

I retained my hold on it and focused on Zane.

He refused to meet my eyes.

"You're an elemental witch," I said to him. "You're here for the same reason I am—to learn how to use your magic." I kept my voice steady, although as I said the words, I knew there was far more to it than that.

When he finally looked at me, his expression was pained.

The woman released a gleeful laugh. "Your boyfriend isn't a witch, a demigod, a water elemental, or whatever he's claiming to be," she said. "He's an immortal."

The moment she said the word, what I'd learned in the scrolls last night rushed through my mind.

The giants.

Strikingly beautiful.

Incredibly strong.

Frost magic.

Immortal.

My feet felt locked to the ground.

Zane created another icicle in his hand and ran at her with an incredible amount of speed.

She readied herself for his attack, and they fought each other with their weapons—her with the dagger and him with the icicle—so quickly that I couldn't keep up with what was happening. It was like they were moving in a blur.

I wanted to send the cheese knife at her again, but they were moving too quickly. I couldn't risk hitting Zane.

Instead, I did the most useful thing I could think to do.

I kneeled to get my phone, texted a pin of our location to Nicole and Alyssa, and messaged them *SOS.*

I looked back up the moment Zane pinned the woman down. But before her back hit the ground, she pulled her arm back and threw the dagger straight at my chest.

I held out my hands and screamed with all the force I

could muster, ready to send it flying back at her the same way I'd turned the crystals on Courtney.

I was too late.

The tip of it collided with my left palm.

But it didn't go through.

Instead, it clanged against my skin, like metal against metal, and fell to the ground.

At the same time, Zane shoved his icicle through the woman's heart.

She disintegrated into ash, the tiny pieces of it spreading around her to join the dirt. Her white jeans and tank top were a pile on the ground.

I stared at the dagger in front of me in shock, then flipped over my hand to study my palm.

There were no marks on it.

How was that possible?

"She's gone," Zane said, hurrying toward me and dropping down on his knees to be level with me. "You're safe now."

He reached for my hands, but I pulled away and stood up, shaking.

He stood as well.

"You knew who she was," I said steadily, sorting through everything I'd just learned in my mind. "And you're not Greek. You're Norse. You're a frost giant."

"I see you learned something last night in the

scrolls," he said, and he sounded almost *proud* of me. "But we call ourselves immortals now."

I reached for the dagger and held it up with the point facing him, as if I'd actually have a fighting chance against him.

His caring eyes flashed with pain. "You don't have to do that," he said. "I'd never hurt you. I just *killed* for you."

"You killed 'one of your own,'" I repeated back how she'd referred to herself earlier.

"She's not 'one of my own,'" he said in disgust.

"Then who is she? *What* is she?"

"Her name is Lin," he said. "She is—*was*—a hand-maiden of Frigg."

"Who's Frigg?"

"A Norse goddess."

"Oh my God." I dropped my arm and the knife fell, too. "I'm right."

I'd *known* I was right. But it felt different to hear it confirmed.

Then I looked back over to the remains of Lin's white clothes.

I should run.

But I'd seen how quickly Zane had moved while he was fighting Lin. He'd catch up with me. And crazily enough, I truly believed he wouldn't hurt me, despite what he was and all the lies he'd been telling me.

I had a sinking feeling it had to do with whatever had happened between us earlier that had made our eyes glow.

I had more questions than I could process.

No running. I needed to keep it together. After all, I'd come out here for answers. These answers were crazier than I'd ever imagined, and I'd somehow almost gotten killed in the process, but I *was* getting them. I wasn't going to stop now.

Knowledge could be more powerful than armor. Especially when used correctly.

I swallowed and tried to get myself together. "Why does a Norse goddess see me as the enemy?" I asked.

"So we're playing twenty questions again," he said with a knowing smile.

"It's not funny," I snapped. "She almost killed me. She *would* have killed me, if I hadn't…"

I trailed off and glanced at the knife on the ground, having no idea how to verbalize what had happened.

"Anyway, yes, I do have questions," I continued. "Lots of them."

"I understand," he said. "But can you promise me one thing?"

"What?"

"I need you to keep all of this secret."

I straightened, instantly on guard. "Why should I do that?"

"For me." His voice was strained, as if I should have already known that. "If they find out what I've been doing here, they'll kill me."

"What *have* you been doing here?" I asked.

"I've been keeping an eye on you all," he said. "To make sure things here stay under control."

"So you're a spy," I realized, the pieces continuing to come together in my mind. "You're Norse, and you're spying on the Greeks."

"It's more complicated than that."

"Which basically translates to yes, you're a spy."

Our gazes locked, and he said nothing—which I took to mean that I was correct.

"I'd never hurt you," he repeated slowly, as if one wrong word would set me off. "You're my soulmate. It shouldn't be possible, but you are. And I'll always protect you, no matter what."

CHAPTER THIRTY-SEVEN

I didn't have a chance to ask anything more, because someone was screaming my name from the woods, his voice getting closer and closer.

Blake.

Nicole must have told him we were here.

I instantly regretted sending that SOS text. Because I was finally getting answers from Zane, and now we'd have to put this conversation on pause until later.

Zane stared in the general direction of where Blake's voice was coming from.

For the first time since meeting him, he looked terrified.

"Don't tell him," he begged, sounding more vulnerable than ever. "If you do, they'll kill me."

My breath caught. Because I had no idea what to do.

If I told Blake the truth, what would happen to Zane?

A pit grew in my stomach at the possibilities. Because despite everything, I didn't want Zane hurt. Or dead. I felt hollow at just the thought of it.

But if I didn't tell the truth, I'd be responsible for keeping Zane's secret, too. I'd become an accessory to his crime.

I'd be turning on everyone at the school. My friends, my teachers… *everyone.*

How was I supposed to do that? Zane might be good at deception, but I was terrible at it.

And I couldn't believe I was even considering it as an option. Because telling Blake the truth was the right thing to do. He and the others would take it from there, and Zane's secret wouldn't become mine to bear.

But if Zane was right in thinking they'd kill him…

At the thought, it felt like someone had taken my heart in their hand and started squeezing it until it was about to burst. Because I'd never be able to forgive myself if that happened.

"Summer," Zane said steadily. "Do this for me. I'll keep you safe. I promise."

Unable to find the words to reply, I swallowed and backed away from him. "Over here!" I called to Blake, and he burst through the trees, holding a fireball in each hand.

He stopped in his tracks when he saw Lin's bloodied clothes and ashes.

"One of them got to you," he said, and the fire he was holding disappeared. "Are the two of you okay?"

"We're fine," Zane said. "She's dead."

"I can see that," Blake said.

"What do you mean by *one* of them?" I asked. "There were others?"

"Eleven of them," he said. "All females. They got through our borders and launched an attack on the students and teachers on campus. They were insanely fast and strong, but we managed to kill them all—except for the one we kept for questioning."

I glanced at Zane, worried. Because if one of them was being kept captive at the school, how would we make sure she kept his secret?

Crap.

I'd just thought of Zane and I as a "we." As if we were in on this secret together.

Which we technically were, until I figured out what I wanted to do.

I had options. I hated both of them, but I had them.

But for now, I needed to focus on what Blake was telling us.

"Was anyone hurt?" I asked him.

His expression hardened, and I knew what his answer was going to be before he said it.

"There were casualties. And many were injured."

"How many?" My thoughts instantly went to Alyssa and Jamie.

"We're still tallying the numbers," he said. "Nicole's trying to heal the ones who were injured, but…"

"Her magic isn't working?"

He glared at me, and I remembered—what had happened Friday night was supposed to stay between the group of us in the cottage. Zane knew nothing about how Nicole hadn't been able to heal my arm.

I could barely keep Nicole's secret.

How was I supposed to keep Zane's?

To his credit, Zane didn't question why I'd think Nicole's magic wouldn't be working. He just stood there silently, giving nothing away.

"Nicole's doing everything she can," Blake said, and then he glanced at the clothes on the ground. "How were the two of you able to kill her on your own?"

Because Zane's an incredibly strong and fast immortal, I thought.

"Instinct, I guess." Zane shrugged. "She interrupted our date. I was pissed."

Anger rushed through me at the fact that he was able to joke at a time like this.

Of course he was. He didn't care about the others at the academy. Maybe Vera, but that was it.

Vera.

Was she an immortal, too?

It would certainly explain how they were "family friends."

"We think they were goddesses of some sort," Blake said, an edge of suspicion in his tone. "It took groups of us to handle each one of them. But there's not a scratch on either of you."

"She threw a dagger at me," I said quickly. "I held out my hands to block it, and it bounced off my palm."

"Huh." Blake's brow furrowed. "That's interesting."

"That was how I was able to kill her," Zane added. "She was so distracted by whatever Summer had done that it gave me an opening."

I refused to look at him. Because I was already helping him keep up his lie, and it hadn't even been ten minutes since learning about it myself.

The pit in my stomach grew, and I continued to ignore Zane, even though the air hummed with whatever connection existed between us.

Soulmates.

Just as quickly as I'd thought it, I pushed the word out of my mind. I'd deal with it—with *him*—later. It was too much to process right now.

"Are you sure it hit your palm?" Blake asked, yanking me out of my spinning thoughts. "Couldn't you have used your air magic to stop it right before contact?"

"It hit my palm. I'm sure of it," I said. "It clanged and bounced off it, like metal against metal."

Blake said nothing for a few seconds.

I couldn't look at either him or Zane. I shifted on my feet, just wanting to get out of the clearing.

I felt Zane glancing at me, but I refused to look back.

"Let's get out of these woods," Blake finally said. "Zane—go back to your dorm once we're back. The surviving students are meeting in their common rooms."

Surviving students.

My throat tightened with worry for my friends, and I prayed they were okay.

"What about me?" I asked.

"You're coming to the cottage with me," he said. "Because Kate will want to hear about all of this."

CHAPTER THIRTY-EIGHT

B lake and I walked the long way back to the cottage.

He said it was because he didn't want me to see the bodies of those who'd died in the attack.

I was grateful for that, because I didn't want to see them, either. Especially if any of them were my friends.

Don't think like that, I told myself. *Alyssa's a great fighter. She knows what she's doing. As does Jamie. They're probably fine.*

I wished I could fully believe it. But I couldn't. Because after what Blake had said about those goddesses, I knew they were powerful enough to take down even the strongest elemental witches.

When we got to the cottage, Kate was waiting inside the living room. There was a pile of books on the coffee table, and she sat on the sofa with one of them open on her lap.

She closed the book and stood when Blake and I entered, looking confused to see me there.

"What's going on?" she asked.

"Summer and Zane were attacked by one of the women in the woods," he said. "They escaped unscathed."

Panic flashed across Kate's eyes. "Where is she?"

"Dead," Blake said simply.

She nodded, satisfied. "I'm glad you found them in time."

"She was dead when I arrived."

Kate looked to me in shock. "How...?" she started, and I shifted uncomfortably, unsure where to begin.

Remember Zane's story, I reminded myself. *He fought her with his magic and killed her while she was distracted by how I'd deflected her dagger.*

Simple. Easy.

If only I didn't feel that gnawing pit in my stomach at the fact that I was going to lie for someone I didn't even think I *liked* more than twenty-four hours ago.

"Summer did something unique with her magic while fighting the woman," Blake said. "I thought you'd want to know about it."

Kate focused on me and tilted her head, curious. "What did you do?"

I recounted what had happened when Lin had thrown the dagger at me. The entire time, I had to remind myself to call her "the woman" instead of referring to her by her name. I only knew her name because Zane had told me. If they knew Zane knew it, they'd become suspicious of him.

As they should be.

Afterward, Kate pressed her lips together, deep in thought.

This was the perfect time to tell her the truth about Zane. How was she supposed to protect the school if she didn't know what we were facing?

Then the desperation in Zane's eyes when he'd begged me to keep his secret flashed through my mind.

If you tell them, they'll kill me.

My heart hurt again at the thought.

"Blake," Kate finally said. "Go help Nicole at the infirmary. Summer—stay here. We need to talk."

Blake gave Kate a single nod, looked at me with suspicion, then left the cottage. The door slammed shut loudly behind him, and Kate and I were left alone.

The back of my neck prickled. Because it didn't feel like we were alone.

I glanced over my shoulder at the bookshelf against the wall, and my eyes went to the gilded mirror hanging above it.

"Is someone watching us?" I asked Kate.

"No." She frowned. "Why would you think that?"

"Occasionally when I'm around mirrors, I can almost swear someone's watching me through them," I said, not realizing how crazy it sounded until after I'd spoken.

She glanced at the mirror, then returned her focus to me. "When did this start?"

"When I got to the school."

"Interesting," she said, pausing before continuing. "I would never condone an invasion of privacy like that, and before today, I would have said it was impossible that anything at this school could be magically tampered with. But those women somehow got past our boundaries. It's quite possible that they've been spying on us. So I'll alert someone about your feeling around the mirrors once we're finished chatting." She motioned to the armchair I'd sat in Friday night. "Right now, I'd like you to have a seat."

I glanced at the mirror one more time before sitting down.

Someone was *definitely* watching us.

Kate was right—it could be the Norse gods. I'd ask Zane next time I saw him. If he wanted me to keep his secret, then he needed to be honest with me about *everything*.

If not…

Could I bring myself to turn him in?

I didn't know. I didn't even know if I was going to keep his secret.

I just needed to get through the rest of the day. Then I could sleep on it and hopefully get a clearer perspective tomorrow.

Kate sat at the edge of the sofa, so she was next to my chair. A quick glance at the book on top of the pile on the coffee table showed she was already on to what was happening.

It was a book on Norse mythology.

I froze, panicked.

Does she know about Zane? Is that why Blake brought me here? She wants to question me about him?

"You look shell shocked," Kate observed. "Under-standably so. After today, I'm feeling the same way."

"Do you know who survived the attack?" I asked quickly.

"Not yet." Her eyes brimmed with concern. "Nicole's going to send me a list once she knows more."

I nodded slowly, trying not to think the worst.

But given that Alyssa or Jamie hadn't texted me yet, it was hard not to.

"In the meantime," Kate continued, and I tried my hardest to focus on her. "I want to chat with you about your magic."

"What about my magic?"

"I already know about the crystals with Courtney, the

targets in archery, and the dumpster in the alley. Now, I need you to tell me about every other instance when you've been able to use it."

I sat back, crossed my legs, and thought over everything that had happened since I'd arrived at Elementals Academy.

"While I was practicing magic with Alyssa, I knocked a bottle cap off a table," I said. "I also made a few crystals float."

Her expression remained neutral. "Anything else?"

Now was the biggie.

"I melted the deadbolt in a door."

"Zane Caldwell's door?"

My heart raced when she said his name, and I swallowed down a lump of anxiety in my throat. "Yes," I said, figuring it would be best to keep it as vague as possible.

The less I said, the less likely it would be that I'd accidentally give something away.

"Blake mentioned having to fix his door," she said. "We assumed it was done by a fire elemental. A very powerful one, at that."

"It was me." I shrugged. "Zane said I probably used my air magic to create a massive burst of heat."

"A burst strong enough to melt metal," she said slowly, like she was contemplating if it were truly possible.

"Apparently so."

I didn't believe it, and judging by her expression, she didn't either.

"So every time you've used your magic, it's been with metal or gems," she said. "Unless you can think of any other instances?"

It was an interesting point, and when I thought back, I realized she was correct.

"I can't," I said. "But when I use my magic, it feels different than what the air students describe. It doesn't feel like I'm connecting with the wind. It feels like I'm connecting with the object I'm controlling."

She gave me a small smile, like she knew something I didn't.

Given that she was a goddess, she clearly knew a *lot* of things I didn't.

"Thank you for sharing all of this with me," she said, sitting straighter. "Because I have a theory, and everything you told me matches it perfectly."

I sat forward, excitement at the possibility of getting some answers thrumming through me. "Tell me."

"There's one god we've never had a descendent or child of before," she started, hesitant at first, but then speaking faster. "It's always been considered a fact that he doesn't involve himself with mortals, especially not romantically. He's commonly known as the god of death, but that isn't true at all. His real affinity is metals and crystals."

"You can't mean…" I trailed off, because compared to the possibility of being descended from any of the other gods, it made a surprising amount of sense.

"I'm referring to the god of the Underworld," she said exactly what I'd been thinking. "Hades."

FROM THE AUTHOR

I hope you enjoyed *The Discovery of Magic!* If so, I'd love if you left a review. Reviews help readers find the book, and I read each and every one of them. They also motivate me to write the next book faster!

To chat with me and other readers about the book, go to facebook.com/groups/michellemadow and join my Facebook group.

The next book in the Elementals Academy series—The Secrets of Magic—is releasing on July 22, 2022.

CONNECT WITH MICHELLE

Never miss a new release by signing up to get emails or texts when Michelle's books come out.

Sign up for emails: michellemadow.com/subscribe
Sign up for texts: michellemadow.com/texts

Social Media Links:

Facebook Group: facebook.com/groups/
michellemadow
Instagram: @michellemadow
Email: michelle@madow.com
Website: www.michellemadow.com

ABOUT THE AUTHOR

Michelle Madow is a *USA Today* bestselling author of
fast-paced fantasy novels that will leave you turning the
pages wanting more! Her books are full of magic,
adventure, romance, and twists you'll never see coming.

Michelle grew up in Maryland, and now lives in Florida.
She's loved reading for as long as she can remember. She
wrote her first book in her junior year of college and
hasn't stopped writing since! She also loves traveling,
and has been to all seven continents. Someday, she hopes
to travel the world for a year on a cruise ship.